I READ THE BOOK
3 humorous screenplays

By

Jeanne "Bean" Murdock

Library of Congress Control Number: 2024916172
ISBN-13: 979-8-9860948-6-1

Front cover image: "Monk Seal" by Jeanne Murdock.
Back cover image: edited by Greg Heller.

The Dubious Detective was originally copyrighted in 2020.
Michelin Man was originally copyrighted in 2020.
Flight Pattern was originally copyrighted in 2019.

TABLE OF CONTENTS

The Dubious Detective **p. 1**
Michelin Man **p. 19**
Flight Pattern **p. 159**

About the Author **p. 303**

THE DUBIOUS DETECTIVE

FADE IN:
APARTMENT, INTERIOR, EVENING

Tony is sitting at his kitchen table
looking at a bunch of papers and hears
a knock at the door.

TONY

Come on in. (Lisa walks in) Hey, Lisa.

LISA

Hi. What are you working on, Tony?

TONY

The sheriff asked me to help out with
an investigation.

LISA

Really? But, he fired you.

TONY

I know.

LISA

You were really irate with him. What
happened in the evidence room wasn't
your fault.

TONY

How was I supposed to know the evidence
room had fire sprinklers?

                    LISA
    Why would they install sprinklers
where's there's paper and other things
easily damaged by water? If there were
a garden down there I could understand.

                    TONY
What else was I supposed to do with the
    electricity out? I had to light a
                   match.

                    LISA
    Exactly. You had to light a match.

                    TONY
   Anyway, we might have another serial
killer on our hands. The sheriff has no
               leads, so—

                    LISA
                How scary.

                    TONY
I'm going to crack the case and get my
job back. I'm a damn good detective. I
           can solve a murder.

                    LISA
Of course you can, dear. So, what's the
                  story?

                    TONY
    Prostitutes have gone missing.

                    LISA
   Where do they hang out anyway?

                     2

                    TONY
              On El Camino.

                    LISA
Ah. I should send my sister down there.

                    TONY
                    Why?

                    LISA
      She's trying to get pregnant. Crack
    whores can get pregnant. Maybe they're
              onto something.

                    TONY
      Has she tried something other than a
        cucumber? (They both laugh)

        LISA (touching envelopes)
              What are these?

                    TONY
      Letters. We think it's the serial
      killer sending me clues as to where
    he's dumped the bodies. I've received
    four over the last eight weeks—the same
    amount of women who have gone missing
        over the same period of time.

                    LISA
                   May I?

                    TONY
              Go right ahead.

                      3

Lisa takes each typed note out of the
envelope and reads to herself.

                    TONY
    I can't make heads or tails out of
                    them.

                    LISA
    What about this one? "It is neither
    golden nor a gate, but it bridges a
                    gap."

          TONY (shaking his head)
    I got nothing. What do you think?

                    LISA
    Oh, I'm terrible at riddles. "It is
    neither golden nor a gate, but it
            bridges a gap."

                    TONY
              Coit tower!

                    LISA
    Maybe something a little longer,
        bigger. "Golden . . . gate."

                    TONY
    The Golden Gate Bridge! (he leans over
    and kisses her) You're brilliant.

                    LISA
    Me? You're the one who figured it out.

                    TONY
    I'll call it in first thing tomorrow
                 morning.

                      4

CUT TO:
APARTMENT, INTERIOR, NEXT EVENING
Tony is sitting at his kitchen table looking at papers, again. He hears a knock on the door.
TONY (in cutesy voice)
Who is it?

LISA (walks in, says in cutesy voice)
It's me. You're in good spirits. What's going on?

TONY
The sheriff just called. They found a body at the bottom of the bay right under The Golden Gate Bridge. It looks like the woman matches the description of one of the prostitutes missing.

LISA
That's great! Congratulations. I mean too bad for the woman, but I'm glad they found her. You did it. You helped find her. See. You're definitely going to get your job back.

TONY
We—I still have three more women to find, not to mention the killer.

LISA (reaching for envelopes, she shuffles them like a deck of cards)
Let's crack another one. Pick a card any card. (Tony picks one, she offers it to Tony)

                    TONY
No, you do the honors. You seem to have
          the magic touch.

                    LISA
No. No. This all you. I'm just reading.
"It's high time you find the next one."

                    TONY
          Read it again.

                    LISA
"It's high time you find the next one."

                    TONY
     High. High. Clouds. Sun. Moon!

                    LISA
Yeah. Yeah. I think you're close. What
     if it has to do with time?

                    TONY
    A watch! The body is in a jewelry
store. Oh, great. There must hundreds
of jewelry stores in the city. Where
          would we start?

                    LISA
What else does time make you think of?
   (she looks up and tilts her head
          towards his clock)

                    TONY
          A clock.

                    LISA
     Oh, good thinking. And that clock is
     pretty high up there. If it were any
         higher, everyone could see it.

                    TONY
       Yeah like if it were on a cloud.

                    LISA
     Not that high. Maybe more like the top
                of a building.

                    TONY
              The clock tower!

                    LISA
     The clock tower. I never would have
              thought of that.

                  CUT TO:
     APARTMENT, INTERIOR, NEXT EVENING
     Tony is sitting at the kitchen table
     looking at papers. Lisa knocks on the
                    door.

                    TONY
     Come in, Lisa. (Tony has a big smile on
                his face)

                    LISA
                    No.

TONY

Yep. A body was found in the basement
of the clock tower. It looks like she
matches the description of one of the
other missing prostitutes.

LISA

Alright! No way. I mean wow. What is
the sheriff saying to you? Is he
starting to come around? Is he showing
gratitude?

TONY (scoffs)

The sheriff only shows his gratitude to
a box of donuts. His holy grail. (they
laugh) What if it's not enough?

LISA

The donuts?

TONY

No. My helping to solve the murders and
find the killer. What if it's not
enough?

LISA

Oh, honey. It will be enough. (she gets
up and walks over to hug him) He'd be
crazy not to take you back.

TONY

But, what if he doesn't?

LISA

What if he does?

                    TONY
            What if he doesn't?

                   CUT TO:
      APARTMENT, INTERIOR, EVENING, ONE
                 WEEK LATER
Tony is sitting at the table looking at
papers. There is a knock on the door.
He pauses several seconds and then gets
         up and answers the door.

                    LISA
What's wrong? Did the sheriff take you
            off the case?

                    TONY
No. I'm still on. Another prostitute
            went missing.

                    LISA
I'm shocked that people miss them.
(Tony gives her a weird look) I mean
            that's terrible.

                    TONY
I just—I was on a roll last week making
good progress and now the guy is a few
         steps ahead of me again.

                    LISA
Oh, I'm sorry. (Tony hands Lisa a
letter) He sent another clue.

TONY
There are two others I still haven't
figured out.

LISA
Well, you don't have to decode them in
order. The dead bodies aren't going
anywhere.

TONY
The bodies will decay.

LISA
Only if they're not eaten by a wild
animal. (Lisa reaches for the new
letter) May I? (Tony nods) "Don't
imprison yourself like a pelican. Don't
imprison yourself like a pelican."

TONY
A pelican? Do pelicans—

LISA
"Don't imprison . . ."

TONY
Marriage! Wedding. The body is in a
chapel.

LISA
Remember after you worked up the
criminal profile you said that the
killer was either Hispanic or at least
spoke Spanish?

                    TONY
                    Yeah.

                    LISA
Look up pelican on your phone. See what
          it means in Spanish.

           TONY (looking at phone)
  P-e-l-. . . Alcatraz. (thinking) He
killed the woman on Alcatraz Island!
But then what did he do with the body?

                    LISA
                    Or.

                    TONY
                    Or.

                    LISA
Or, maybe the body is on (prompting
               Tony)—

                    TONY
           On Alcatraz Island!

                    LISA
You're my hero. I don't know how you do
     it. I'm terrible at riddles.

                    TONY
        It just takes practice.

CUT TO:
APARTMENT, INTERIOR, NEXT EVENING

Lisa knocks on the door.
TONY (sitting at table)
It's open. (Lisa walks in with a bag of food) Hey, Lisa.

LISA
I bought Chinese. I hope that's OK.

TONY (gasps)
Are you thinking what I'm thinking?

LISA
I asked for extra soy sauce.

TONY
That, too. Maybe the serial killer is Chinese.

LISA
Is there such a thing as a Chinese serial killer?

TONY
Maybe in China. Well they found a woman's body on the shore of Alcatraz Island, and it looks like she, too, matches the description of a missing prostitute.

LISA

Wow. You're definitely getting your job
back. Let's celebrate with yummy food
and decoding the other two clues.

TONY

After dinner, if we have time. (gives
Lisa a sly look)

LISA

Oooh. Well, maybe we don't even have
time for dinner. (Tony stands and walks
up to Lisa and starts kissing her. Then
he lifts her up and puts her on the
kitchen counter.) So soon? We've only
been dating two months.

TONY

The prostitutes have the night off.
(They both laugh)

Tony and Lisa make love.

CUT TO:
APARTMENT, INTERIOR, NEXT MORNING

TONY (sitting at a table, holding up a
piece of paper)
What's this? (Lisa goes wide-eyed) I
called this into the sheriff. They
found another body. How did you know
where the body was? Are you the one who
has been sending these clues? Are you
the serial killer?

LISA
No, God no.

TONY
And to think I made love to you last
night.

LISA
Well if it makes you feel any better I
faked the orgasm.

TONY
You can do that? (Lisa looks at him in
surprise that he didn't know girls did
that) It doesn't matter. Are you the
serial killer? Have you been sending
these clues?

LISA
Yes. No. No. No.

TONY (jumps and stumbles from chair,
points gun at Lisa)
Which is it?

LISA
No, I'm not the serial killer. Yes,
I've been sending you the clues.

TONY
If you're not the serial killer then
how do you know where the bodies are?
Are you his accomplice?

LISA
No.

14

                    TONY
            You're his shrink!

                    LISA
        No. I said I'm a manicurist.

                    TONY
            What's the difference?

                    LISA
I know where the bodies are because I'm
an intuitive. (Tony gives her a look of
confusion) I'm an intuitive. You know
              an intuitive.

                    TONY
    Oh. Prove it. Make this fork move.

                    LISA
That's telekinesis. I'm an intuitive. I
  sense things before they happen. And
even dream them. (Pointing to paper) I
saw her in a dream and wrote myself a
  note, forgetting I wasn't at home.

                    TONY
If you're an intuitive, then prove it.
            Sense something.

    LISA (closes her eyes, concentrates,
            then opens her eyes)
      Your mom's about to call.

                (a few seconds pass, Tony's phone
                             rings)
                TONY (looks at phone, wide-eyed)
              It's my mom. She never calls before
             noon. Alright. Then if you're so good
             at this in-tu-bation, who's the serial
                             killer?

                              LISA
              I've been . . . I can see that he's a
             man, but I'm having trouble seeing his
                             face.

                              TONY
                             Think.

                              LISA
                   I can't force it to come.

                              TONY
                             Think.

                              LISA
              OK OK. Can you at least put the gun
             down so I can concentrate? (Tony puts
            the gun down on the table) (Lisa closes
             her eyes for several seconds and gives
             a big sigh to relax, then she opens her
              eyes widely and drops her jaw) It's
               you. It's you. You're the serial
                     killer. Oh, my God.

Tony slowly reveals Lisa's right and gives an eery smile and gives four, slow creepy claps.

THE END

MICHELIN MAN

FADE IN:
SAN FRANCISCO SKYLINE, LATE
AFTERNOON

CUT TO:
ALAMO SQUARE PARK WITH "PAINTED
LADIES" VICTORIAN HOMES IN
BACKGROUND, SAME

FADE IN:
EXTERIOR, ONE VICTORIAN HOME, SAME

Michelin Man a.k.a. Michael Mann walks home from work. He walks down the street toward his house and sees his stuff flying out of the second-story window. One by one he sees a tire thrown out, four total. His girlfriend Rebecca throws them and screams.

REBECCA
Tires (tire flies out window) don't (2nd tire thrown) belong (3rd tire) in the bedroom (4th tire thrown).

MICHAEL (looks up, dodges tires)
Rebecca, sweetie. What are you doing?

Michael watches each tire bounce and roll down the street of San Francisco.

                        REBECCA
                  It's over, Michael!

                        MICHAEL
            How did you get into my apartment?

                        REBECCA
               You gave me a key, remember?!

                 MICHAEL (under his breath)
                       I guess I did.

                        REBECCA
            Who keeps tires in the bedroom?!

          Rebecca throws out a tire iron.

                        MICHAEL
            When did you learn how to change a
            tire? I thought you had no interest in
                          cars.

            REBECCA storms out the front door.
                   Goodbye, Michael.

                        MICHAEL
            Wait. Sweetie. What'd I do wrong?

                        REBECCA
            If you don't know, then you don't
                     deserve me.

          Michael sulks down the street, passing
          Neighbor Number 1 and Neighbor Number
            2, who figure out what happened.
          Michael fetches the tires, one by one

                           20

rolling each up the street and carrying it up the stairs to his apartment.

CUT TO:

INTERIOR, VICTORIAN HOME, SAME
Michael is in his bedroom and sees his bed up on blocks. He puts the tires back on his bed, which looks like a child's bed—a car bed. Michael uses an impact wrench.

SIX MONTHS LATER

CUT TO:

EXTERIOR, STREET LEVEL, VICTORIAN HOME, LATE AFTERNOON

The same scene happens as with Rebecca. Michael stands on the sidewalk and this time his girlfriend Joanne screams and throws the tires out the window.

JOANNE
What (1st tire thrown out) is your (2nd tire thrown) fascination (3rd tire thrown) with tires (4th tire thrown)?!

MICHAEL
Joanne, honey. What are you doing?

Michael watches each tire bounce and roll down the street of San Francisco.

                    JOANNE (throws tire iron)
              I wasted enough of my life with you,
                          Michael.

                    MICHAEL (under his breath)
                 What'd I do wrong this time?

                 JOANNE storms out the door.
                      Goodbye, Michael.

           Michael doesn't even bother to stop
         her. He performs his familiar ritual of
         fetching each tire. He passes Neighbors
                       1, 2, and 3.

                    NEIGHBOR NUMBER 3
                   (to other 2 neighbors)
                      What's going on?

                    NEIGHBOR NUMBER 1
                       Bad break-up.

                    NEIGHBOR NUMBER 3
                  Oh. But why the tires?

                    NEIGHBOR NUMBER 2
                      We don't know.

                        CUT TO:
         EXTERIOR, MICHELIN STORE, MORNING,
                      8:45 a.m.

                        CUT TO:
         INTERIOR, MICHELIN STORE, SAME

The store is open Monday through
Friday, 9 a.m. to 5 p.m.

Michael sulks into store, walks into
his boss, Darnell's, office and sits in
a chair.

DARNELL
Hey. What's up? What? Not again.
Already?

MICHAEL
Joanne broke up with me.

DARNELL
Ah, I'm sorry, man. What happened?

MICHAEL
I don't know. I guess I'm just unlucky
in love. I waited 30 years to start
dating. I really wanted to get it
right, but I can't seem to make it past
the three-month mark. I fell in love
with Joanne. I really thought that she
was the one. Then, again, I thought
that with Rebecca, too. What am I doing
wrong?

DARNELL
Look. You're not doing anything wrong.
You just haven't found the right one,
yet.

MICHAEL
What are the red flags I missed? When
am I going to see the checkered flag?

23

DARNELL
Well, neither one liked watching car
races with you or going to car shows.
And they didn't know anything about
cars. Their idea of checking tire air
pressure was driving up to our shop and
honking their horns. Not that we mind
checking.

MICHAEL
Not that we mind checking. When did you
know Ginny was the one?

DARNELL
Well, from the beginning, but that
wasn't the same for her. No, sir. She
liked me and all, but I made a lot of
mistakes. There were *many* times I
almost lost her.

MICHAEL
How did you get her to fall in love
with you?

DARNELL
I just kept trying to do better and
better, ya' know? And somehow,
eventually, she loved me *because of* my
weaknesses. She's a saint.

Darnell and Michael stand up and walk
toward the front of the store.

                    MICHAEL
I'm worried that I won't get it right
next time and I'll be doomed to be
       Michelin Man forever.

Michael takes his spot on the platform.
The clock strikes 9 a.m. and Michael
becomes inanimate—Michelin Man—the
store mascot/logo. Darnell turns the
       CLOSED sign to OPEN.

NEIGHBOR NUMBER 1 walks into store and
passes Michelin Man and does a double
       take at Michelin Man.
              (to Darnell)
        He looks familiar.

                   DARNELL
He gets that a lot. He has one of those
                   faces.

             NEIGHBOR NUMBER 1
                   Yeah.

Neighbor Number 1 moves to a section of
   the show room to look at a tire.
Customer Number 1 walks in store and
passes Michelin Man. She looks back at
                    him.

             CUSTOMER NUMBER 1
                   Cute.

Customer Number 1 looks ahead and
Michelin Man raises his left eyebrow
      showing interest in her.

DARNELL
Welcome. How can I help you?

CUSTOMER NUMBER 1
I need new tires for my car.

DARNELL
Do you know what kind you want?

CUSTOMER NUMBER 1
Rubber? (she gives a look like she
knows nothing about cars)

DARNELL
Ah. Why don't you meet me at the
computer?

Customer Number 1 walks to the counter
while Darnell shakes his head at
Michael.

8 HOURS LATER

Clock strikes 5 p.m. All of the
customers are gone. Michael becomes
human and steps off the platform.

MICHAEL
(to Darnell)
Did you see her?

DARNELL
See who?

                    MICHAEL
You know. The woman who called me cute.

                    DARNELL
Yeah, I saw her. Slow down. Remember.
Take it slowly. You need to get this
                next one right.

                    MICHAEL
You're right. I'm just ready to move on
  with my life. I'm tired of selling
tires. I need more meaning in my life.
I want to sell a whole car. What was
                she like?

                    DARNELL
Let's just say that when I asked her
what size tires she needed she said,
                "Double D."

MICHAEL (with big smile on his face)
                    Oh?!

                    DARNELL
    No. (don't even think about it)

                    MICHAEL
Alright. I'm going to take off. See you
                  Monday?

                    DARNELL
              I'll be here.

        Michael walks out door.

                      27

CUT TO:

INTERIOR VICTORIAN HOME, MORNING
Michael is in his car bed, slowly
waking up. He goes into the bathroom
and comes out a couple of minutes
later. Michael walks downstairs to get
the paper and then goes to his kitchen
to eat breakfast (cereal with dried
fruit, orange juice) and to read the
paper. He reads the business section
first. Done with his morning routine,
Michael watches car racing for a couple
of hours and then heads out for a walk.
Every person he passes looks at him as
though he looks familiar.

CUT TO:

EXTERIOR VICTORIAN HOME, SAME,
AFTERNOON

NEIGHBOR NUMBER 4 (to Michael)
Hi. You look familiar. (Michael worries
that she recognizes him as Michelin
Man) Aren't you . . . you're that . . .
that director. What's his name? I know!
Michael Mann (Michael is relieved).

MICHAEL
Oh, yes. My name is Michael Mann.

NEIGHBOR NUMBER 4
I knew it!

                    MICHAEL
Well, no. My name is Michael Mann, but
    I'm not the famous director.

                NEIGHBOR NUMBER 4
                  You're not?

                    MICHAEL
No. Have a nice day. (He walks on)

Michael comes upon a disabled vehicle,
   hazards flashing, flat tire. He
immediately notices the brand of the
                    tire.

         MICHAEL(under his breath)
   Should have bought a Michelin.
(to the female driver freaking out and
  looking at the flat tire, trying to
  call for help) Hey. It looks like
you're having a rough day. (Michael
         finds her attractive)

                FLAT TIRE GIRL
   Yeah. Can you help? I don't know
        anything about cars.

                    MICHAEL
                 Absolutely.

   Michael changes the tire.

                FLAT TIRE GIRL
Thanks so much. Can I buy you a coffee?

Michael is conflicted. He wants to go
out with her—she's beautiful—but she's
not right for him. She doesn't even
know how to change a tire. She's not
right for him, and he wants to hold out
for true love.

                    MICHAEL
        No, thanks. I don't do drugs.

                FLAT TIRE GIRL
                    Huh?

                    MICHAEL
Go to the Michelin store on Monday and
buy a new tire. Tell 'em Michael sent
you. They'll take good care of you.

                FLAT TIRE GIRL
        Well, Michael. Thank you.

                    MICHAEL
            You're welcome.

Michael continues down the street and
then turns down a road where there are
several auto dealerships. He daydreams
about selling a whole car one day—maybe
even owning a business. He stops at the
Chevrolet dealership and fancies the
Corvettes, equipped with stock Michelin
                    tires.

EXTERIOR, CHEVY DEALERSHIP, SAME

                    Car Salesman SAL
                  Hi. Can I help you?

                        MICHAEL
              Hi. I'm just looking around.

                         SAL
          You look familiar. (Michael worries
        that he's recognized as Michelin Man)
          Aren't you that guy? I've seen you
        before. You're . . . Oh! Michael Mann—
                    the director.

                 MICHAEL (relieved)
            Oh. I get that a lot. My name is
        Michael Mann, but I'm not a director.

                         SAL
        I can get you a real good deal. Isn't
                  she a beauty?

                        MICHAEL
                     For sure.

                         SAL
        You can take the Misses for a drive up
                    the coast.

                        MICHAEL
                 I'm not married.

SAL
Boy will you turn heads driving this
Corvette around. (leans in and talks
softly) Sometimes I (air quotes) borrow
one of these on the weekends. It's a
real chick magnet if you know what I
mean.

MICHAEL
What's the torque?

SAL
It's a V8. (pauses, nods, as though he
answered the question correctly) Let me
show you the engine. (he lifts the
hood—no engine, lifts the trunk—no
engine) Well, you get the idea.
(Michael shakes his head, knowing that
it's a mid-engine vehicle) Would you
like to take it for a test-drive? Don't
worry. It handles real nice. I'll walk
you through it. Or should I say drive
you through it. Ha ha.

MICHAEL
Sure. Why not?

They get in the car and Michael zooms around the streets of San Francisco like he's at Le Mans. He even jumps a couple of intersections. Sal holds onto the chicken-shit bar with his right hand and has his left hand on the dashboard, fearing for his life. Everyone they pass stops and takes notice of the Corvette flying past. At the end of the joy ride, Michael burns rubber in the dealership parking lot, parks, they step out.

MICHAEL takes a big breath.
Ahhh. Nothing like the smell of new Michelin tires. (Sal nods and gestures and tries to speak. He's disheveled and traumatized, but tries to play it off.) Well, I sure do appreciate you letting me test drive the C8. You're right. She sure is a beauty . . . and a head-turner. See ya' 'round. (Sal waves and still tries to speak)

CUT TO:
INTERIOR MICHELIN STORE, MORNING

MICHAEL walks into the store at 8:45 a.m. and heads for Darnell's office and sits.
Hey, man. How are you? How was your weekend?

DARNELL
Good. You?

MICHAEL
I test drove the new Corvette C8. Ah,
man!

DARNELL
Ah, man! How was it? Does it have our
tires?

MICHAEL
Yes! It was sweet! It handles nicely
and grips the road like a banker with
your money. I met Sal.

DARNELL
Oh, no. What happened? That guy is a
piece of work.

MICHAEL
Yes. He doesn't know a cylinder from a
test tube. (They both laugh)

DARNELL
That guy is such a dipstick.

MICHAEL
Then, he should know where it is! (They
both laugh)

DARNELL
That guy is so dumb, he doesn't even
know that he's dumb.

MICHAEL

The only thing he should be selling is scales—the only thing he can weight/wait on. (They both laugh) How's Ginny? What did you two do last weekend?

DARNELL

Everything's good. Ginny and I went to one of those couples' cooking classes.

MICHAEL

Really? You hate to cook.

DARNELL

I know. It wasn't so bad though. This is what I've been trying to tell you. Sometimes you gotta try new experiences and do what your lady wants in order to keep her happy. You gotta find ways to tighten the connection, strengthen the bond. It's when you give *your* interests more time than a *lady's* interests that she starts to get bored with you, maybe even stray. Ya' know?

MICHAEL

That makes a lot of sense.

DARNELL

Who knows? I might even lose a few pounds (pats belly) now that I'm a better cook.

MICHAEL
Wow. You really are in love. I met
someone last weekend.

DARNELL
What happened?

MICHAEL
I helped a lady change her flat tire.
She was really pretty—

DARNELL
Hold it. Hold up. Hold it. (Darnell
leans forward) Do you even hear
yourself? You helped her change a flat
tire.

MICHAEL
Yes.

DARNELL
She doesn't know about cars.

MICHAEL
Oh, I know. Nothing happened. We didn't
go out.

                    DARNELL (leans back)
Oh, thank God. I'm worried you're going
to go down that same track. You need to
   have things in common with a girl
  before you decide to date her. Then,
  you need to see if you even like her
    and enjoy spending time with her.
   Finally, she may look great on the
   outside, but what's under the hood?
   (Michael gives a sly smile) No, you
   nimrod. What's under the hood is what
   matters most. Ya' know? Her soul.

                    MICHAEL
     Ahhh. (Michael nods and ponders
          Darnell's wise words)

                    DARNELL
          Now let's get to work.
  They head to the front of the store.
   Darnell turns the CLOSED sign to OPEN
     and Michael takes his place on the
                   platform.

Customer Number 2 walks in store and
passes Michelin Man. She looks back at
  him and then looks forward. Michelin
 Man raises his right eyebrow showing
           interest in her.

        CUSTOMER NUMBER 2 (to Darnell,
        gesturing toward Michelin Man)
        Handsome guy. Is *he* for sale?

                    DARNELL
             Uh, well. I . . .

CUSTOMER NUMBER 2
I'm kidding. He's probably more
interesting than any guy I've
dated . . . and more faithful.

DARNELL
If you only knew.

CUSTOMER NUMBER 2
Excuse me?

DARNELL
Uh, huh.

8 HOURS LATER

The clock strikes 5 p.m. All of the
customers are gone and Michael steps
off the platform and walks up to
Darnell. Michael takes a breath before
commenting on the cute girl.
DARNELL interrupts him.
No.

MICHAEL (dejected)
Alright. Do you need help with
anything? Can I help you lock up?

DARNELL
No. You just go home and take a cold
shower.

MICHAEL
I'll see you tomorrow.

DARNELL
See ya', man.
Michael walks home; he doesn't own a car, because there is no place to park in San Francisco and he lives close to work. He also likes to walk. On his way home, he stops at a bookstore to check out the latest car books.

CUT TO:
INTERIOR, BOOKSTORE NAMED LIVRES, SAME, LATE AFTERNOON

Bookstore Worker MARYANNE
Hi, Michael.

MICHAEL
Oh, hey, Maryanne. How are you? How's business?

MARYANNE
It's booming. People still read. Can you believe it?

MICHAEL
"One can never know too much; the more one learns, the more one sees the need to learn more and that study as well as broadening the mind of the craftsman provides an easy way of perfecting yourself in the practice of your art."
[Auguste Escoffier]

MARYANNE
You're a wise man.

                    MICHAEL
              Auguste Escoffier.

                    MARYANNE
         Oh. The French chef. So, what'll you
         have, today? The usual? I have a few
         new car books. You know where to look.

                    MICHAEL
                    Thanks.

         Michael walks to the car section and
         peruses the new selection. He opens a
         book and flips through it. At one point
         Michael looks up from the book to
         ponder what he read. A sign catches his
         eye. Michael does a double take. "SELF
         HELP." He's conflicted as to whether or
         not to satisfy his curiosity. Michael
         looks around to make sure that no one
         sees him. He grabs a book and flips
                    through it.

MICHAEL

*Successful Dating at Last! A workbook
for understanding each other.* That's
what I need. You have one more chance,
buddy. You have to get it right. (He
scans the table of contents, running
his finger down the page) What I value
in myself. What I value in others. My
dating resume. Ha! (his finger
continues down) Sex. This should be
interesting. (he flips to the chapter
called Sex, the audience doesn't see
the pages, he closes the book and nods,
he walks to the front of the store)

MARYANNE

What'd you find? (Michael sets the book
on the counter) Oh. (Maryanne doesn't
say anything else because she wants to
stay professional, she really wants to
say something though, Michael gives her
money) This one's on the house, Dear.

MICHAEL
What? No.

MARYANNE

I insist. You've helped me so much at
Mich—I mean you told me to go to
Michelin and they've helped me so much
over the years (she knows he's Michelin
Man, he doesn't know she knows).

MICHAEL
Oh. Wow. Well, thank you, Maryanne. I
guess I'll see you next time.

MARYANNE
Goodbye, Dear.

Michael walks out of the store.
CUT TO:
STREET OF SAN FRANCISCO, SAME
Michael continues toward home and
passes an elementary school where there
is a group of teachers out front saying
bye to each other. Michael eyes one,
Patricia, who feels someone looking at
her. She looks back and smiles at
Michael. Embarrassed that he was caught
looking at her, he quickly looks down.

CUT TO:
INTERIOR, MICHAEL'S APARTMENT,
SAME, EVENING
Michael turns on the TV to a reality
show about car restoration. He sits
with his new dating book and flips
through it. Michael jots notes in it,
since it is a workbook. After an hour
he gets up and puts it in his bookcase,
which is all car and business books.

CUT TO:
INTERIOR, MICHAEL'S APARTMENT,
NIGHT
Michael is sitting in bed reading
another self-help book.

CUT TO:
STREET OF SAN FRANCISCO, MORNING

Michael walks to work, passing the elementary school. Patricia is in the school yard with the kids. She notices him, but he doesn't notice her because he's reading another self-help book. Michael passes the bookstore, also.

CUT TO:

INTERIOR, BOOKSTORE, SAME

MARYANNE
He'll get there.

CUT TO:

EXTERIOR, STREET LEVEL, VICTORIAN HOME, DAY

Michael walks out of his home and heads down the street, reading another self-help book. He passes Neighbors 1, 2, and 3. They notice the title: *Last Chance, Buddy*. They look at each other in judgment. Michael doesn't notice them and keeps walking. Then he passes another damsel in distress with a flat tire, but he doesn't notice.

ONE YEAR LATER

CUT TO:
INTERIOR, VICTORIAN HOME, MORNING
Michael is eating breakfast while
reading yet another self-help book. He
notices the time and gets up to go to
work. Michael walks to his bookshelf
and places his most recent installment
in his collection. The bookcase is now
all relationship and other self-help
books.

CUT TO:
INTERIOR, MICHELIN STORE, SAME,
AFTERNOON

Patricia finishes her business in the
store and then walks toward the exit
and stops at Michelin Man. She touches
his face and looks back toward Darnell.

PATRICIA
He seems so real.

DARNELL
He is.

PATRICIA
What?

DARNELL
He is . . . to us.

44

PATRICIA
Hmm.

Patricia walks out. Michelin Man
slightly raises his eyebrows and looks
like he's in love. The clock strikes
5 p.m. and Michelin Man comes to life.

MICHAEL (to Darnell)
It's her! That's her, Darnell!

DARNELL
Mmm. Hmm.

MICHAEL
I'm serious. I felt it when she touched
me. Did you see her touch my face?!
What's her name?

DARNELL
Patricia. Now don't you go—

MICHAEL
I won't. Have a good night.

Michael runs out of the store and out
to the parking lot.

CUT TO:
EXTERIOR, MICHELIN STORE, PARKING
LOT, SAME

MICHAEL (to Patricia, at her car)
Excuse me. Patricia.

45

PATRICIA turns around.
Yes.

MICHAEL
Hi. (points to self) Michael. I, uh,
just wanted to thank you for your
business.

PATRICIA
Oh, you're welcome. You look familiar,
but I don't remember seeing you in the
store.

MICHAEL
Oh, I was in the back doing inventory.
So, thanks, again, and let me—us—know
if you need anything else. We have
air . . . and it's free.

PATRICIA
Thank you. I will.

MICHAEL
(under his breath, walking back toward
store)
We have air . . . and it's free?
Stupid. Stupid. I'll never find true
love talking like that.

6,000-8,000 MILES LATER

CUT TO:
INTERIOR, MICHELIN STORE, DAY

Patricia walks in and caresses Michelin
Man's left arm as she passes him. He
looks like he melts and he's excited
she's back.

PATRICIA
(to Darnell)
Hi. Is Michael here?

DARNELL
Oh, uh. He stepped out.

PATRICIA
Do you know when he'll be back?

DARNELL (looking down)
No.

PATRICIA
I'm Patricia. I need to get my tires
balanced and rotated and I was hoping
to talk with Michael while I waited. He
was so nice last time I was here.

DARNELL (looks up)
Oh, Patricia. I remember you.

PATRICIA
You do? You must have a lot of
customers.

DARNELL
We do. Uh huh. But it's easy to
remember a beautiful woman. (he looks
at Michelin Man who gives Darnell a
dirty look for flirting with Patricia)

PATRICIA
Aw. You're sweet. Well, uh. I guess
I'll just sit and wait. Here are my
keys.

DARNELL
We'll have you back on the road in a
jiffy.

PATRICIA (hoping to be there long
enough to see Michael)
No hurry.

Patricia sits in the showroom and just
looks around. Michael looks at her
longingly. Every time Patricia looks at
him he resumes a straight face.

DARNELL (to Patricia)
Alright, Miss. Your car is all set.

PATRICIA
That was fast. You're sure you don't
need to do anything else?

DARNELL
No, ma'am. You're good to go.

PATRICIA (delaying)
Alright. Well, see you next time.

DARNELL
We'll be here.

Patricia walks out of the store. The clock strikes 5 p.m., and Michelin Man becomes human.

                    MICHAEL (to Darnell)
                    Darnell! She—

                    DARNELL (begrudgingly)
                    Go ask her out.

                         CUT TO:
EXTERIOR, MICHELIN STORE, PARKING
               LOT, SAME

Michael runs out the door and catches Patricia at her car. He stops and is out of breath from being nervous.

                         MICHAEL
                    Hi, Patricia!

                         PATRICIA
Michael! I was hoping to see you here.

                         MICHAEL
                         Oh?

                         PATRICIA
Yes. You were so nice last time. I just thought, I just figured I'd see you again.

                         MICHAEL
I just came out to make sure everything is OK with your car.

PATRICIA
Seems so.

MICHAEL
(long, awkward pause) Great. (he waves
and turns and walks toward store, and
then turns toward her, and then turns
toward store, and then walks back to
her) I don't normally ask out customers
but (looks off knowing that's a
lie) . . . would you like to go for a
water some time?

PATRICIA
Well, I don't know. Water on a first
date? What are you trying to take
advantage of me? (Michael looks
embarrassed, she slaps him on the
shoulder) I'm kidding. I'd love to go
for a water with you.

MICHAEL
Great. Great. Water it is.

PATRICIA
How about I meet you here Saturday?
Noon work for you?

MICHAEL
Sure!

PATRICIA
We can drink from the hose. (Michael is
perplexed, but agreeable) I'm kidding!

                    MICHAEL
                  Oh, right.

         PATRICIA (she runs her hand down his
                       arm)
        I'll see you then. (she gets in her car
        and drives off, he waves and acts cool)

        When Patricia is out of sight, Michael
        collapses on the ground and lies in the
        spread eagle position looking up at the
                  sky. She melts him.

           DARNELL (walks out of store toward
               Michael and steps over him)
        I guess she said yes. Remember, take it
         slow. (still looking down at Michael)
                  See ya' later, Romeo.

                    SATURDAY
        CUT TO: EXTERIOR, MICHELIN STORE,
                    AFTERNOON
        Patricia drives up and parks. Michael's
        waiting for her. She steps out of the
                 car and greets him.

                    MICHAEL
        Hi, Patricia. Thanks for being on time.
                  You look nice.

                    PATRICIA
                  Hi. So do you.

MICHAEL
I thought we could go to Cafe Du Monde.
We can walk. Are those shoes OK for
walking?

PATRICIA
Oh, yes. It's San Francisco. I know not
to wear heels. (they start walking) I
went to the Cafe Du Monde in New
Orleans. I've seen the one here, but
I've never been.

MICHAEL
It's by my house.

PATRICIA
Where do you live?

MICHAEL
I'm in one of the Painted Ladies.

PATRICIA
Oh, I've always wanted to live in one
of those. Well, I have a view of them.
I live on the other side of the park.

MICHAEL
No kidding. I'm surprised we haven't
seen each other.

PATRICIA
Maybe we have. (They walk up to
Livres.) Do you mind if we pop in? I
want you to meet someone.

MICHAEL (pointing to the sign)
Livres.

PATRICIA
Yes. It means books in French.

MICHAEL
I know.

CUT TO:
INTERIOR, BOOKSTORE, SAME

PATRICIA
Hi, Aunt Maryanne.

MARYANNE
Patricia. What a nice surprise. Hi,
Michael.

PATRICIA (to both)
You two have met?

MARYANNE
Michael is one of my regulars. Quite
the intellectual.

MICHAEL (to Patricia)
You're related.

PATRICIA
Maryanne is my mom's sister. In my
family the women are all into books—
writing them, selling them, or teaching
from them.

MARYANNE (to Michael)
Patricia's a teacher. I guess you
already know that.

MICHAEL
No, we didn't get that far.

MARYANNE
Well, you don't have to go much
farther. She teaches right next door.

PATRICIA
Alright. I'll fill him in on the rest.
I just wanted to pop in and say hi.

MARYANNE
Glad you did. You two have fun. I know
you will.

PATRICIA and MICHAEL
Bye. (they walk out)

CUT TO:
EXTERIOR, BOOKSTORE, SAME

MICHAEL
So, you're an elementary school
teacher.

PATRICIA
Yes. I teach 5th grade. I love it.

MICHAEL
I was going to ask you if you had any
kids and now I know the answer.

PATRICIA
Twenty.

MICHAEL
Do you have any kids of your own?

PATRICIA
No, but I would like to some day. How
about you?

MICHAEL
I don't have any kids. I would like to
have kids, but I don't know if I can
have any.

PATRICIA
What makes you say that?

NEIGHBOR NUMBER 5 (to Michael)
Oh, hey. Hi. Aren't you that guy
(Michael looks worried) . . . I've seen
you on TV . . . what's his name . . .
Oh! Michael Mann! (Michael is relieved)
The director.

MICHAEL
My name is Michael Mann, but I'm not
the director. See ya', man. (they walk
on)

PATRICIA
What was that about?

MICHAEL
Mistaken identity. I get that a lot.

PATRICIA
Huh. Michael Mann. I can see the
resemblance. You *are* handsome.

MICHAEL (blushing, they walk up to the
cafe)
Would you like to sit outside or in?

PATRICIA
Outside. It's so nice out. (she sits
down)

MICHAEL
I'll get us drinks. Do you prefer flat
or bubbly?

PATRICIA
Flat, like my chest. (she laughs)

Michael looks at her chest and then
blushes for doing so. He walks into
cafe and then comes out with two
waters.

PATRICIA
So, I have an important question to ask
you. (Michael looks worried) Why water?

MICHAEL (relieved)
Water is the fountain of youth. What
else would be in a fountain?

PATRICIA
I like it. So, how long have you worked
for Michelin?

                    MICHAEL
          All my life, it seems like.

                    PATRICIA
      I know what you mean. I feel like I
      live at school. What are you working
          toward? What's your goal?

                    MICHAEL
      I like tires; I really do. I just, I'm
       ready to sell a whole car. You know
      what I mean? My dream is to own a Chevy
                  dealership.

                    PATRICIA
      No kidding?! Corvette is my favorite
      car. When I was growing up my dad owned
                    a '63.

             PATRICIA and MICHAEL
                 Split window!

                    PATRICIA
                 Sorry, go on.

                    MICHAEL
      No. I want to hear more about the split
      window. Does your dad still have it?

                    PATRICIA
      He would if it had fit in the casket
                  with him.

                    MICHAEL
        Oh, I'm sorry. Is your mom still
                    living?

PATRICIA
No, she's gone, too. It's just Aunt
Maryanne and me. Are your parents still
around?

MICHAEL
No. Mine are dead, too. Can we get back
to the '63?

PATRICIA
Please.

MICHAEL
What happened to it? Please tell me you
have it.

PATRICIA
I have it.

MICHAEL
Ahh! Maybe for our next date you can
pick me up in it. We can take a drive
and then go to the Chevy dealership and
check out the new C8.

PATRICIA
Our next date?

MICHAEL
Oh, well. I don't mean to be
presumptuous. I just—

PATRICIA
I'd love to go on another date with
you, Michael.

MICHAEL (blushes, changes the subject)
Tell me more about teaching.

PATRICIA
I love it. The kids are really great. I
love watching them grow during the
year, not just physically, of course.
You know when we were kids, 6th grade
was the last year of elementary school,
but now it's the start of middle
school. I like the challenge of getting
the kids ready for the next stage in
their lives. It's a big jump.

MICHAEL
It is a big jump. Wow. I love your
passion. The kids are lucky to have
you.

PATRICIA
Thanks. Speaking of kids. You said that
you want kids, but you don't know if
you can have them.

MICHAEL
Oh, uh, you don't know unless you've
tried, right?

PATRICIA (nodding)
Right. Sorry. I don't mean to pry. It's
just that the clock is ticking if you
know what I mean.

MICHAEL
I do know. I want control of my life.
And more than anything connection. I
want to have that connection that comes
with something you own, like a
business. I want to connect with people
on a deeper and more long-lasting level
than what I get at the store. I want
the passion that you have with
teaching.

PATRICIA
It sounds like you want love. (Michael
blushes) Well, that's what passion is,
right? That's why it feels so good.
Whether your passion is surfing,
painting, writing, reading, you lose
yourself in it. You forget about time.
There isn't anything you'd rather be
doing and you have no care in the
world. Same with making love to
someone. (Michael blushes) It's OK.
It's natural. Everyone wants love. (She
puts her hand on his)

MICHAEL
You're right. I guess I shouldn't be
embarrassed about it.

PATRICIA
No. I want love, too. (She looks at her
watch) Listen, can we continue this
conversation another time. I have
papers to correct.

                    MICHAEL
        Sure. Of course. (They stand) Is your
          offer still good to take me for a
                      drive?

                    PATRICIA
        Is your offer still good to take me on
        a second date? (She laughs) Of course.
                  Let's head back.

        They walk back toward the store and
          pass the bookstore. They wave at
                    Maryanne.

                    CUT TO:
            INTERIOR, BOOKSTORE, SAME

        Maryanne looks toward window and waves
             at Michael and Patricia.

                    CUT TO:
        EXTERIOR, MICHELIN STORE, SAME

                    MICHAEL
          I had a nice time. I enjoy your
                    company.

                    PATRICIA
            I had a nice time, too.

                    MICHAEL
            Same time next week?

                    PATRICIA
              Sounds good.

Michael leans in and gives her a kiss
on each cheek.

PATRICIA
Au revoir.

MICHAEL
Bye.

CUT TO:
INTERIOR, MICHELIN STORE, MORNING

Michael walks into Darnell's office and
sits. Michael is on a cloud with every
waking and sleeping thought about
Patricia.

DARNELL
I take it the date went well. (Michael
dazed, nods) What'd you do?

MICHAEL
Uh huh.

DARNELL
Wow. Maybe this girl is different. I've
seen you infatuated, but not like this.
Did you—

MICHAEL
No. Darnell, she owns a 1963 Corvette.

                    DARNELL
     Split window. Nice. OK, now we're
     getting somewhere. Does she have a
     sister? (Michael gives a look) I'm
            kidding. Tell me more.

                    MICHAEL
       Remember Maryanne from Livres?

                    DARNELL
                     Sure.

                    MICHAEL
        Maryanne is Patricia's aunt.

                    DARNELL
          No kidding? Small world.

                    MICHAEL
     We went to Cafe Du Monde, speaking of
      world. Anyway. Patricia teaches 5th
      grade. (zones out, looking off) I'm
      going to marry her, Darnell. I am. I
     promise I won't rush into it. I'm just
     telling you I know. I'm going to marry
                      her.

                    DARNELL
          What if she wants kids?

                    MICHAEL
      I already know she does. But I don't
                know if I—

DARNELL
I know. Just take it one step at a
time. Remember first see if you have
enough things in common with her then
see if you continue to enjoy spending
time with her. (Michael nods, dazed,
looking off full of enchantment) Oh,
boy. We gotta bleeder! (as in bleeding
heart)

Darnell walks out of the office to open
the shop and leaves Michael behind.

CUT TO: EXTERIOR, MICHELIN STORE, DAY
Patricia drives up in her 1963 'vette.
Michael stands outside of the store
watching her drive up.

MICHAEL
I'm in love.

PATRICIA (stops next to Michael, peers
out and up to him standing by the
passenger door)
Hi, Michael. So, what do you think?

MICHAEL
Gorgeous.

PATRICIA
And what do you think about the car?
(Michael blushes) Get in.

CUT TO: INTERIOR, 1963 CORVETTE, SAME

PATRICIA
Have you eaten lunch, yet? I packed a
picnic.

MICHAEL
No. Sounds good.

PATRICIA
I found out that there's a classic car
show at Harmony Park. We could have
lunch and then walk around. Does that
sound OK?

MICHAEL
Sounds perfect. (they drive off,
Patricia drives to the park like she
too could compete at Le Mans, they have
a casual conversation as though this
driving is just a stroll for them) So,
how was your week? Were your kids on
their best behavior?

PATRICIA
Yes, they were great. It's always
exhausting, but I love it.

MICHAEL
How did you get into teaching?

                    PATRICIA
Like I said, some of the women in my
family were teachers. I guess I was
            born into it.

                    MICHAEL
        I know what you mean.

                    PATRICIA
            How about you?

                    MICHAEL
Same. (they arrive at park, Michael
looks at Patricia like he's even more
in love because she knows how to drive,
then looks at all the cars) Oooh. (he
looks like a kid in a candy store)
                    Nice.

                    CUT TO:
        PARK, GRASSY AREA, SAME

Michael and Patricia are sitting on a
        blanket, eating lunch.

                    PATRICIA
Ah. It's so nice out. Ha. Look at that.
  People are looking at my car. (she
pretends to yell) It's not part of the
show. I should tell them it's for sale.

                    MICHAEL
    What?! You want to sell your car?

PATRICIA
Everything's for sale for the right
price.

MICHAEL
I like how you think. Mmm. Lunch was
great. Thank you. Are you ready to walk
around?

PATRICIA
You're welcome. Sure.

Patricia and Michael put the picnic
basket in the 'vette and peruse the car
show. A little girl runs up and gives
Patricia a hug.

PATRICIA (to little girl)
Hey, Lacy. (Lacy runs back to her dad,
Patricia waves to Lacy's dad) Hi!

MICHAEL
One of yours?

PATRICIA
Yes.

MICHAEL
She loves you. I bet all your kids are
like that.

PATRICIA
I'm pretty lucky.

MICHAEL
I don't think it's luck.

PATRICIA
Look! The Chevy dealership has a booth.
Let's go mess with Sal.

SAL
Step right up, Folks. Check out the new
C8. It's everything you've ever wanted
in a car. Comfortable, sporty, stylish—

PATRICIA and MICHAEL
Hey, Sal. Remember us?

SAL
Hey how ya' doin'? (he's racking his
brain, he doesn't remember anyone
because everyone is just a number to
him)

MICHAEL
Remember what you said about the C8
being good for picking up chicks? (Sal
racks his brain, he can't keep his bull
shit straight) You were right. I got
this hot babe (Michael puts his arm
around Patricia's waist) and now we're
engaged.

SAL
Yeah right. Wow. I remember. (he
doesn't) See. Yeah. The C8 answers your
prayers. It's a real man's car.

PATRICIA
I saw Michael test driving the C8 and I
thought: I'm going to marry him.

SAL
See. Now let's get you locked in at a
low interest rate and you can go home
with this beauty.

MICHAEL
See ya'.

Michael and Patricia walk away and Sal
is still rambling with his sales pitch.

MICHAEL moves his arm up to Patricia's
shoulders and looks at her.
I already have my beauty. (Michael
drops his arm, Patricia smiles and puts
Michael's arm back around her waist)

CUT TO:
EXTERIOR, VICTORIAN HOME, SAME,
NIGHT
Michael and Patricia are sitting in her
car outside of Michael's home.

PATRICIA
(quoting Sal) It's a real man's car.
(They both laugh) Aaah. I had fun
today.

MICHAEL
Me, too. Can I see you tomorrow?

PATRICIA
That would be nice.

                    MICHAEL
I'll call you in the morning. (he leans
  over and kisses her on the cheek)
                   Bonsoi.

                   PATRICIA
                    'night.

After kissing Patricia on the cheek,
Michael has a flash to walking down the
street past the elementary school and
seeing a beautiful woman talking with
              other adults.

                   MICHAEL
               That was you.

                   PATRICIA
Whom did you think you were kissing
               goodnight?

                   MICHAEL
No that was you in front of the school
with the group of teachers. I realize
  that was the first time I saw you,
   rather than at Michelin. I know you
don't know what I'm talking about. You
 wouldn't have noticed me, but I just
   realized. I was walking by and—

Patricia has a flash to a memory of
         Michael walking by.

PATRICIA
Oh. Yes. I remember. I turned around
and we caught eyes for a moment. I
thought you looked familiar when I saw
you at Michelin.

MICHAEL
I never forget a beautiful face. (he
gives her one more kiss on the cheek
and gets out of the car)

CUT TO:
EXTERIOR, NAIL SALON, DAY

Michael and Patricia walk out of a nail
salon admiring their hands.

PATRICIA
Well, that was a first for me.

MICHAEL
What do you mean? You said you've been
here before.

PATRICIA
Yes, but not with a guy. Not on a date.

                    MICHAEL
I'm open to experiencing what you like
to do. Things that are novel to me.
Besides, I enjoy spending time with
you. And look at these nails. (he holds
his hands up) Forget owning a car lot.
I want to be a hand model. (they laugh)
     Hey. Do you want to go back to my
place? We can have lunch and catch the
              end of the race.

                    PATRICIA
   I thought you'd never ask. I've been
    wanting to see the interior of a
             Painted Lady.

                 CUT TO:
     INTERIOR, VICTORIAN HOME, SAME

                    PATRICIA
                     Wow!

                    MICHAEL
             This is home.

                    PATRICIA
             So beautiful.

                    MICHAEL
             It's comfortable.

                    PATRICIA
   I should say. The architectural detail
   is exquisite. More beautiful than I
                expected.

                    MICHAEL
          Can I get you anything to drink?

                    PATRICIA
     I can wait 'til lunch. Look at the
                    view.

                    CUT TO:
          PARK ACROSS THE STREET FROM
             PAINTED LADIES, VIEW FROM
              VICTORIAN HOME, SAME

                    CUT TO:
        INTERIOR, VICTORIAN HOME, SAME
             They walk up the stairs.

                    MICHAEL
             This is the bedroom.

                    PATRICIA
     A car bed! No way! I had one as a kid.
     (Michael embarrassed) No, I love it.
     I've been tempted to get one, again,
     but you know. I thought it might be a
     mood killer. Guys already don't like
     that I know more about cars than they
                  do. I figured—

                    MICHAEL
     I know. I can't exactly say that it's
        won me Brownie points. What's so
        immature about having a car bed?

                    PATRICIA
          Nothing. It's practical.

                       73

MICHAEL
It's practical.

PATRICIA
Well, I like it. May I? (she lies down
on the bed) Aah. Comfy. (she pats on
the bed for him to join her)

MICHAEL (lies down next to her, stiff
as a board, they stare into each
other's eyes, Patricia is hoping he'll
kiss her, he jumps out of bed)
Well. Better get those sandwiches
ready.

CUT TO:
LIVING ROOM, VICTORIAN HOME, SAME

Michael and Patricia are sitting on the
couch in front of the TV watching a
race and eating sandwiches. They lean
forward and cheer.

MICHAEL
Yes! Michelin tires get another
checkered flag.

PATRICIA
That was great. Did you see? He almost
lost it at the end.

MICHAEL
I know.

Patricia and Michael lean back to recover from the excitement of lunch and a race. They stare into each other's eyes and Michael finally makes the first move by kissing Patricia. He pauses to ponder his cross-roads. Michael only has one more chance to fall in love and make it work. Is Patricia the right one? Is she worth the risk? He resumes kissing her and tries to go all the way.

PATRICIA
Wait.

MICHAEL
I'm sorry. I know this is only our third date. You're just so beautiful and I—

PATRICIA (pointing up)
The car bed.

MICHAEL
Really.

PATRICIA
Oh, yeah.

Michael leads her up the stairs, into his room, and lays her down on the bed. They make love.

CUT TO:
INTERIOR, MICHELIN STORE, MORNING

Michael walks into Darnell's office and
sits down. Darnell is sitting at his
desk.

DARNELL
Wow. I didn't think you could look any
more starry-eyed. I think I see Orion.

MICHAEL
We spent the whole weekend together.

DARNELL
Nice. So—

MICHAEL
Yes.

DARNELL
Alright. OK. Cool. But, can you two
relate to each other?

MICHAEL
We had so much fun. We went to a car
show. We watched a race on TV.

DARNELL
That's good and all, but did you do
anything she likes?

MICHAEL
That's the thing. She likes all that.
Oh, you'll love this. You'll be so
proud of me. Sunday we had a manicure.

DARNELL (shocked)
Alright. Now we're gettin' somewhere.
(Michael holds his hands out to display
his new-found look, then he holds them
up to himself, he stares as though he
can see Patricia's beautiful face in
his nails)

MICHAEL
Darnell, do you believe in love at
first sight?

DARNELL
With fingernails?

MICHAEL
Now I know for sure I fell in love with
Patricia the first time I saw her.

CUT TO:
INTERIOR, BOOKSTORE, DAY

MARYANNE
So, how are you and Michael getting
along?

PATRICIA
Great. He's so nice and so cute and so
sweet. And ambitious. I finally found a
guy with goals.

MARYANNE
Oh, that's great, dear. I'm so happy
for you. You two seem good together.
Michael's a good guy.

PATRICIA
Michael is so interesting. There's
something about him that seems worldly.

MARYANNE
Maybe he has traveled.

PATRICIA
I don't know. We haven't talked about
that, yet. He seems . . . French.
Didn't you say that our ancestors came
from France?

MARYANNE
Yes. Not your dad's side, though. Just
your mom's. Our grandparents immigrated
from France.

PATRICIA
Right. Oui. Hmm. Maybe Michael and I
are related. Oh, no!

MARYANNE
You're not related. But, I do see
something special between you two.
Michael's been a customer for several
years. I thought that you two would be
a good match—

PATRICIA
Why didn't you tell me? Why didn't you
introduce us?

MARYANNE
Well, you know, dear, sometimes you
just have to let nature take its
course.

PATRICIA
You're right. Timing is everything.
Well, I'm going to stop by Michelin and
say hi to Michael.

MARYANNE
Do you think that's a good idea? Maybe
you should call first. He might be
busy.

PATRICIA
I'm sure he won't mind.

CUT TO:
INTERIOR, MICHELIN STORE, DAY
PATRICIA walks by Michelin Man and
gives him a big smile. She looks ahead
and he smiles, too.
(to Darnell) Hi, Darnell. Is Michael
here?

DARNELL
No, he stepped out, Patricia.

PATRICIA
OK. Well—

DARNELL
It sounds like you two have been having
a lot of fun together.

PATRICIA
Michael talks about me?!

DARNELL (wide-eyed)
Mmm hmm.

PATRICIA
That's nice. OK. Well. I guess I'll
just catch him another time.

DARNELL
Yeah. It's better to catch him outside
of work hours.

PATRICIA
That's what I'm gathering.

CUT TO:
INTERIOR, '63 VETTE, DAY
Michael is driving Patricia's car north
across the Golden Gate Bridge. They
look at each other and smile. He puts
his right hand on her left knee and
then back on the steering wheel.

EXTERIOR '63 VETTE, DAY, GOLDEN
GATE BRIDGE, SAME

CUT TO:
FISHERMAN'S WHARF, SAME
Patricia and Michael are standing at
the side of a pier looking out at the
water. They kiss.

CUT TO:
EXTERIOR, CAFE DU MONDE, SAME
Patricia and Michael are sitting
outside having lunch.

CUT TO:
WOODS, HIKING TRAIL, DAY
Patricia and Michael stop to rest and
drink water. Patricia kisses Michael
and touches him all over.

MICHAEL
What? Here?

PATRICIA
You're not afraid of a little poison
oak, are you?

MICHAEL
It would be worth it.

THREE MONTHS LATER

CUT TO:
SEBRING, FLORIDA, SUNDOWN

CUT TO:
HILLTOP, SEBRING, FLORIDA, SAME
Sound of corvette.
Michael and Patricia share binoculars.

MICHAEL
I can't believe it. Sure enough.
They're already testing another
Corvette.

PATRICIA
Bolide! We don't need binoculars to
know that. Wow.

MICHAEL
Sweet. Have you ever driven on a race
track, before?

PATRICIA
Once. Before my dad died we took the
'63 to Buttonwillow. It was the last
item on his bucket list—race on a road
course.

MICHAEL
Awesome. Did you get to drive?

PATRICIA
Yes, but my dad had to wait on the
sidelines. He was easily car sick and
was already experiencing nausea.

MICHAEL
Oh.

PATRICIA
How about you? I bet you've driven on
many tracks.

                    MICHAEL
Yes. It's one of the perks of working
              for Michelin.

                   PATRICIA
        What's your favorite track?

                    MICHAEL
         That's easy. Talladega.

                   PATRICIA
              Oh. nice.

                    MICHAEL
        I prefer the oval tracks.

Michael points the binoculars at
Patricia. I like this view better. He
puts the binoculars down and kisses
         her. They lie back.

                    MICHAEL
        Je t'aime, Patricia.

                   PATRICIA
      I love you, too, Michael.

                    MICHAEL
I want you to be my girlfriend. There
isn't anyone I'd rather be with.

                   PATRICIA
I feel the same. I want you to be my
girlfriend. (they laugh) I thought
you'd never ask. You're so sweet.

MICHAEL
And you're so beautiful and intelligent
and with such a joie de vivre.

PATRICIA
It's easy to be excited about life when
I'm with you.

They kiss. The sun sets. The Corvette
can still be heard.

SIX MONTHS LATER

CUT TO:
INTERIOR, MICHELIN STORE
8:55 a.m.

MICHAEL (walking to the platform,
answers cell phone)
-Hi, Patricia.

CUT TO:
INTERIOR, CLASSROOM, SAME
KIDS ARE DOING INDEPENDENT WORK

PATRICIA (quietly by the door)
-Hi, Michael.
-Sorry to bother you. I know you're
about to open the store.

CUT TO:
INTERIOR, MICHELIN STORE, SAME

MICHAEL
-That's OK. I have a couple minutes.
What's up?

CUT TO:
INTERIOR, CLASSROOM, SAME
PATRICIA
-I need to talk to you.
-It's important.
-I think I might be—

CUT TO:
INTERIOR, MICHELIN STORE, SAME
Michael sees a customer walking up to
the door. The CLOSED sign is still
showing.

MICHAEL
-Sorry, Patricia. I know I said I have
a couple minutes.
—I see a customer walking up. I should
go.
—I'm sorry. I know you said it's
important.
—Can we continue this when I see you
tonight?

CUT TO:
INTERIOR, CLASSROOM, SAME

PATRICIA (disappointed)
-Sure. I understand.
-It's OK.
-I guess it's better that we talk in
person.
-No, it's OK.
-I'll see you tonight.
-Bye.
(to her class)
Who wants to write Mississippi on the
chalk board?

Many children raise their hands.

CUT TO:
INTERIOR, VICTORIAN HOME, SAME,
EVENING
Michael and Patricia are eating dinner.

PATRICIA
So, I still need to talk to you. (long
pause)

MICHAEL
Oh, right. Yeah. I'm sorry. Sorry I
couldn't talk earlier. Sorry I forgot.
It was crazy today. You said there was
something important. Is everything OK?

PATRICIA
Michael, I think—

MICHAEL
Oh, no. I know. I know where this is
going. I've been a terrible boyfriend.
I should be more attentive. I should—

PATRICIA
No, no. It's nothing like that. No,
you've been great.

MICHAEL
I have?

PATRICIA
Of course. I love you, Michael. (she
touches his hand)

MICHAEL (relieved)
Oh, thank goodness. I would never want
to do anything to hurt you. I don't
want to lose you. I love you with all
my heart.

PATRICIA
I know you do. What I have to tell you
is that I think—

MICHAEL
Oh, my gosh. Did something happen to
the Corvette?

PATRICIA
No.

MICHAEL
Did something happen to one of your
kids? Did you lose your job?

PATRICIA
No, no.

MICHAEL
Is Maryanne OK?

PATRICIA
Yes, she's fine. Michael. I think I
might be pregnant.

MICHAEL
Pregnant?! How. What if.

Michael worries that his offspring will
also have to be Michelin Man and go
through all that he has. He puts his
fork down and decides he lost his
appetite. Michael picks up his plate
and takes Patricia's while she grabs as
much as she can. She wasn't done
eating. Also, it looks like she has a
big appetite. Is she eating for two?
Michael puts the plates in the kitchen
sink and leans over. Big sigh. Patricia
walks up to him and puts her hand on
his back.

PATRICIA
Are you going to be OK? I don't even
know for sure. I have an appointment
tomorrow morning with my OB/GYN.

MICHAEL
I can't—

                    PATRICIA
              I know. It's OK.

                    MICHAEL
              I don't even—

                    PATRICIA
   Let's take one step at a time. OK? I'm
   sorry this happened. I must have. This
   isn't like me. I'm so organized. Before
   getting pregnant, it would be like me
    to have the baby's name picked out,
    school district—that's an easy one,
     crib assembled, be on pre-natal
   supplements. And I would schedule it so
      that the baby is born in June.

    Michael gives the slightest laugh.

                    PATRICIA
    Whatever happens it'll be OK. I
   promise. OK? Please look at me. (he
   looks at her, they kiss) OK? (he nods)
              I should go.

                    MICHAEL
       I'll walk you to the door.

             At the door.
                    MICHAEL
   Call me after work and let me know how
         the appointment went.

                    PATRICIA
      I will. Bye. I love you.

MICHAEL
I love you, too.

Michael shuts the door and walks to his
bookcase. He looks at his options to
determine which book could help him
through this hurdle. Which book could
have prevented this hurdle? He sees
none and plops on the couch and turns
on the TV and zones out at a car race.

CUT TO:
INTERIOR, MICHELIN STORE, MORNING
Michael walks past Darnell. Darnell
turns and watches Michael walk past.

DARNELL
Hey, man. What—. Michael.

Michael walks into Darnell's office and
plops into the chair. Darnell meets
Michael in the office and sits.

DARNELL
Geez, man. What happened to you? You
look like you just saw a ghost. You
look shell-shocked. Is everything OK?
Hello. Anyone home?

MICHAEL
Patricia's pregnant.

                    DARNELL
Whoa. Oh. Now that news would make even
   me White. I don't know what to say,
      man. What are you going to do?

                    MICHAEL
      She's going to tell me tonight.

                    DARNELL
  Oh, so you don't even know for sure.

                    MICHAEL
      She has an appointment with her
   gynecologist right after school.

                    DARNELL
  Are you going? Oh. (realizes Michael
 will still be inanimate at that time)

                    MICHAEL
Darnell, what am I going to do? What
                    if—

                    DARNELL
I know. I know. Just take one step at a
   time. Talk to her tonight and then see
               what happens.
     Michael nods and gets up and walks
             toward platform.

                   CUT TO:
      INTERIOR CLASSROOM, SAME
  CHILDREN ARE DOING INDEPENDENT
                   WORK

Patricia sits at her desk staring off.
A child is raising his hand for help.
Patricia doesn't notice. His arm is
getting tired. The kids look at the boy
and at Patricia. They wonder what is
wrong with Patricia.

CUT TO:
EXTERIOR, CLASSROOM, SAME
Principal does a double take and stops
at Patricia's closed door and looks
through window and notices Patricia
staring off and boy with raised hand.
The boy and the principal catch eyes.

CUT TO:
INTERIOR, CLASSROOM, SAME
The boy with the raised hand shrugs
toward the principal. The principal
walks in.

PRINCIPAL EDWARDS
Miss Leblanc.

PATRICIA
Oh. Principal Edwards. Class, say
"Hello, Principal Edwards."

ALL STUDENTS
Hello, Principal Edwards.

PRINCIPAL EDWARDS
Is everything OK?

PATRICIA
Everything is great. Yes. Thanks for
checking in. (to class) Let's get
started on math.

The principal walks out.

CUT TO:
INTERIOR, GYNECOLOGY OFFICE, EXAM
ROOM, SAME, AFTERNOON

Patricia is in a hospital gown sitting
on an exam table. (inaudible) The
doctor tells her she's not pregnant.
Patricia nods. (audience doesn't know
the result)

CUT TO:
EXTERIOR, GYNECOLOGY OFFICE
INTERIOR, '63 VETTE, SAME
Patricia calls Michael and leaves a
message.

PATRICIA
—Hi, Michael.
—I guess you're busy.
—Please call me back.
—I just had my appointment with the
gynecologist.
—OK.
—Love you.
—Bye.

CUT TO:
INTERIOR, MICHELIN STORE, SAME
Michael steps off the platform, and
Darnell turns the OPEN sign to CLOSED.
Michael listens to his voicemail.

PATRICIA
Hi, Michael. I guess you're busy.
Please call me back. I just had my
appointment with the gynecologist. OK.
Love you. Bye.

DARNELL
Well.

MICHAEL
She didn't say.

DARNELL
Call her back.

MICHAEL (puts phone in his pocket)
I will when I get home.

DARNELL
Don't torture the poor girl.

MICHAEL
See you tomorrow.

CUT TO:
INTERIOR, VICTORIAN HOME, SAME,
EVENING
Michael sits on his couch. He picks up
phone and listens to voicemail.

PATRICIA
Hi, Michael. I guess you're busy.
Please call me back. I just had my
appointment with the gynecologist. OK.
Love you. Bye.

Michael looks at Patricia's missed call
and is about to push Dial and decides
to put the phone back down instead and
to go to bed. He leaves his phone on
the couch. When Michael is upstairs, he
misses another of Patricia's calls.

CUT TO:
EXTERIOR, ELEMENTARY SCHOOL, DAY
Teachers walk into the school. Patricia
calls Michael.

PATRICIA
-Hi, Michael.
-I tried reaching you last night.
-I guess you were busy.
-I really need to talk to you.
-I have the results from the (tries not
to let others hear her) test.
-Love you.
-Bye.

CUT TO:
INTERIOR, MICHELIN STORE, SAME
Michael is inanimate on the platform
and feels his phone vibrate. He gets a
worried look on his face.

CUT TO:
INTERIOR, VICTORIAN HOME, MORNING
Michael sits up in bed and looks at his
phone. He sees several more missed
calls and decides to listen to the ones
he didn't listen to earlier in the
week.

PATRICIA
(one message) *Michael it's me. I don't
know if there's something wrong with
your phone. I've been trying to reach
you all week.* (skips to next message)
*Michael, I need to talk with you about
my test results—in person.* (skips to
next message) *Is everything OK? I'm
really worried about you. Please call
me and at least tell me you're alive.
I'm sorry about all this. I love you.*

Michael is about to dial Patricia's
number and chickens out again. He puts
the phone down, goes into the bathroom,
and then goes outside to get the paper.
He runs into Patricia who is about to
knock on his door.

MICHAEL
Patricia!

                    PATRICIA
Michael! Oh, thank God. (she hugs and
kisses him, he gives a cold response)
You're alive. What's going on? What
  happened? I thought something bad
  happened to you. Are you OK? Why
haven't you returned any of my calls?

                    MICHAEL
  Oh, uh. I was just about to stop by
              your house?

                    PATRICIA
In your pajamas? What's going on? I've
been trying to tell you the result of
  my pregnancy test. Don't you care?

                    MICHAEL
Of course I care. Of course I care. Let
              me just. OK.

                    PATRICIA
          I'm not pregnant.

                    MICHAEL
           Oh, thank God.

Michael collapses to the ground and
  lies spread eagle looking up at the
sky. Neighbors 1, 2, and 3 walk by and
   assume he's having relationship
            problems again.

PATRICIA
Michael, please get up. You're
embarrassing me. (he gets to his knees
and puts his head into the front of her
thighs) Get up.

MICHAEL
Come in.

Michael takes her into the dining room
and pulls out a chair for Patricia and
then he sits in another chair. She
stays standing.

PATRICIA
Michael, now that I know you're OK I'm
angry with you. How could you do that
to me? Last week was hell. Not only did
I have to deal with the possibility of
being pregnant but also the thought of
having to raise the child by myself.
You abandoned me when I needed you
most.

MICHAEL
I know. I know. I was scared. I
thought—

PATRICIA
How do you think I felt? Did you even
stop to think how I felt? Do you care?

MICHAEL
Yes, yes of course I care. I care. I
love you.

PATRICIA

Well, you sure haven't been acting like
it. What are you so afraid of? You're
not the one who would have to carry the
baby for nine months and then breast
feed for a year. You would have it
easy.

MICHAEL

You're right. You're right. I'm just
afraid—

PATRICIA

What? What are you so afraid of? Why
won't you tell me? Why won't you talk
to me? You know that you can tell me
anything. Don't you trust me?

MICHAEL

Yes, of course I trust you. I'm just
not ready to have children yet.

PATRICIA

Well, I'm not either. We're not even
married.

MICHAEL

We're not even married. We should be
doing things in order.

PATRICIA

Right. We should be doing things in
order.

MICHAEL

We met. We fell in love.

PATRICIA
Check. Check.

MICHAEL
Maybe we should just slow things down a
bit and focus on getting to know each
other better.

PATRICIA
Yes. Right. Get to know each other
better. (awkward silence) I'm going to
go.

MICHAEL
Meet you later for lunch? Cafe Du
Monde?

PATRICIA
Yes, sure.

MICHAEL
I'll walk you to the door.

PATRICIA
Don't get up. I'll see myself out.

EXTERIOR, CAFE DU MONDE, SAME,
AFTERNOON

Patricia and Michael sit at their usual
table. They don't talk or look at each
other. They just pick at their food.

EXTERIOR, CHEVY DEALERSHIP, SAME

Patricia and Michael walk by Chevy
dealership where Sal is outside
wheeling and dealing a couple.

SAL (to man)
A few trips around the block in this
beauty and you won't be needing those
little blue pills if you know what I
mean. (elbows him) huh, huh. (to
Patricia and Michael, couple run off)
Hey, Folks. Heya. Hi. Over here. The
new Corvette is ready for you to test
drive. Walk on over I'll be with you in
a bit. (he looks around and doesn't see
couple) Or right now.

Patricia and Michael are oblivious to
Sal and aren't talking with each other.

CUT TO:
GOLDEN GATE BRIDGE
EXTERIOR, '63 VETTE, SAME, EVENING

CUT TO:
INTERIOR, '63 VETTE, SAME

Patricia drives and Michael is in the
passenger seat. They are quiet and just
look straight ahead.

CUT TO:
EXTERIOR, '63 VETTE, SAME

Patricia drives like a Sunday driver
and everyone passes her.

CUT TO:
EXTERIOR, VICTORIAN HOME, SAME
Patricia drops off Michael at his home.

MICHAEL
I had a nice time.

PATRICIA
Yes, me too.

MICHAEL
Well. I'll see you—

PATRICIA
I'm going to have a pretty busy week.
Maybe we should just talk next weekend.

MICHAEL
Oh, OK. My week's looking pretty full,
too. (he gives her a kiss on the cheek)
Love you.

PATRICIA
(she nods) Bye.

INTERIOR, VICTORIAN HOME, SAME

Michael walks up stairs into his
bedroom.

102

MICHAEL
(stands in front of his bed) Maybe I
should save her the trouble and take
the tires off and throw them out the
window. Then I would be of use to her.

Michael opens the window and looks down
at the street. No one is there. He
looks out at the park. Michael grabs
his impact wrench and looks out the
window one more time. He spots
Patricia's car as she drives back home.
Michael puts the wrench down and sits
on the bed.

EXTERIOR, CAFE DU MONDE, DAY

PATRICIA
So, how was your week?

MICHAEL
Good. We sold a lot of tires. How about
you?

PATRICIA
Good. Good. Good. The kids were great
as usual. I had a lot of papers to
grade. That's about it.

MICHAEL
That's great. How's Maryanne?

PATRICIA
She's well. Still selling lots of
books.

MICHAEL
I haven't been in there in a while. I
should stop and say hi.

PATRICIA
Why don't we stop by after lunch.

MICHAEL
That's a great idea.

PATRICIA
How's Darnell?

MICHAEL
Oh, he's still Darnell. He's a good
manager. I have a lot of respect for
him. He's a good friend, too. He and
Ginny have quite the love affair.

PATRICIA
Yes. It's a beautiful thing. (Patricia
stares off wishing she had quite the
love affair and thought she did and
wonders what happened)

Michael stares off with the same
thoughts.

MICHAEL
Oh, I spoke to the owner of the Chevy
dealership. Not Sal, of course. Can you
imagine him keeping any business
afloat? (they laugh) He might be
interested in selling the company to
me.

PATRICIA
(somewhat apathetically) That's great.
Wow. You're really doing it. I'm happy
for you.

MICHAEL
Yes, well, we'll see. I haven't signed
the papers, yet. And I have a lot of
things to get in order first. (he has
to be permanently animated)

PATRICIA
I have some news, too. I was offered a
principal job.

MICHAEL
Patricia, that's wonderful. I remember
you saying that you wanted more
responsibility. And you'll still get to
be around the kids.

PATRICIA
Yes. It's a really good offer. It's in
New York City.

MICHAEL
Oh, wow. New York. That'll be
different. Congratulations.

PATRICIA
I haven't accepted the offer, yet. I
wanted to think about it and talk with
you, of course.

MICHAEL
If that's what you really want you
should definitely take it.

PATRICIA
(changing the subject) It's supposed to
rain tomorrow and I just washed my car.

MICHAEL
Rain in California in May? I guess if
you ever want it to rain you should
just wash your car.

PATRICIA
Native Americans have it all wrong.
Instead of dancing they should wash
their cars.

MICHAEL
You mean their horses.

PATRICIA
Is that a racial slur?

MICHAEL
No. This is a racial slur. (slurred)
Native American.

They laugh. Then awkward silence.

PATRICIA
Well, shall we?

MICHAEL
I'm full.

They walk to Livres.

CUT TO:
EXTERIOR, LIVRES, SAME

Patricia and Michael wave to Maryanne.

CUT TO:
INTERIOR, LIVRES, SAME

MARYANNE
Patricia, Michael. This is a nice
surprise. (she immediately notices that
something is different)

PATRICIA
Hi, Aunt Maryanne.

MICHAEL
(to Maryanne) Hello. (to Patricia) I'll
be in the back, dear.

MARYANNE
Is everything OK, dear?

PATRICIA
Yes, everything is fine. I'm full. We
just ate at Cafe Du Monde.

MARYANNE
Très bon.

PATRICIA
(big sigh) So, how are you?

MARYANNE
Tired. Getting older. I don't know how
much longer I can do this.

PATRICIA
Are you still thinking about selling?

MARYANNE
Thinking about it. I don't have anyone
to pass it down to.

PATRICIA
I know. I'm sorry. I—

MARYANNE
Don't apologize. You're meant to teach.
And you have that principal job offer.
Did you and Michael talk about it?

PATRICIA
Not really. I told him.

MARYANNE
How did he take it?

PATRICIA
You know. He's always supportive.

MARYANNE
Is everything OK between the two of
you, dear?

PATRICIA
Yes. I think we're both just tired.

MICHAEL
(walks back to the front of the store,
holds up a book) Starting a business
for morons.

PATRICIA
It sounds like you would be a moron for
starting a business. (to Maryanne) No
offense.

MICHAEL
Is everything OK?

PATRICIA
Yes, I was just saying that we've been
tired.

MARYANNE
Be patient with each other.

Michael pays and he and Patricia walk
out.

MARYANNE
Take care, you two.

MICHAEL AND PATRICIA
Bye.

CUT TO:
EXTERIOR, VICTORIAN HOME, SAME

Michael and Patricia walk into
Michael's home.

                         CUT TO:
          INTERIOR, VICTORIAN HOME, SAME
      Michael and Patricia sit at the dining
      table. Michael peruses his new book.

                        MICHAEL
          Deciding what to offer. Chevrolets.

                        PATRICIA
                     That's easy.

                        MICHAEL
      Market research. Financing. Accounting.
                  Customer service.

                        PATRICIA
                  You have that down.

                        MICHAEL
         Legal matters. Distribution. Human
                     resources.

                        PATRICIA
                Keep Sal. Dump Sal.

      Patricia isn't really interested, since
        things aren't good between them.

                        MICHAEL
      Well, I don't want to bore you. I can
               look at this later.

                        PATRICIA
                  I don't mind.

MICHAEL
Let's see if there's a race or car show
on.

Michael puts the book in his bookcase
and they move to the couch. They stare
at the TV unenthusiastically and
zombie-like.

MICHAEL
A blow-out already? Should have used
Michelin.

PATRICIA
You've said that before.

MICHAEL
I could be a great race car driver.

PATRICIA
If that were true you'd be one already.

MICHAEL
It wouldn't be any fun now having chick
racers. Women don't belong on the
track. Auto racing is a man's sport.

PATRICIA
Excuse me. So, you wouldn't support me
if I wanted to race? You've seen how I
am with the '63. I'm a great driver.

MICHAEL
For a girl.

PATRICIA
What?!

MICHAEL
You know what I mean.

PATRICIA
No. Please enlighten me. You're being a
jackass.

MICHAEL
I'm sorry. I don't know why I said all
that. (Patricia stands up, Michael
holds her arm and gently pulls her back
down) Please stay. I love you.

Michael kisses Patricia. At first she
doesn't kiss him back and then she
does. This is the first they have been
intimate in a while. She is frustrated,
but she also misses the intimacy. They
start going all the way on the couch.

MICHAEL
Ow.

PATRICIA
Oh, sorry.

MICHAEL
(trying to unbutton Patricia's dress) I
can't—

PATRICIA
That's OK. I'll do it. Do you have a
condom?

                    MICHAEL
Be right back. (Michael runs up stairs
and comes back down with a condom, he
sits on the couch and is about to open
    the packet) I'm scared. What if
            something goes wrong?

                   PATRICIA
Nothing went wrong before. I wasn't
        pregnant. We'll be fine.

                    MICHAEL
    OK. (he sets the condom down)

        They go back to kissing.

                   PATRICIA
    I don't like that, remember?

                    MICHAEL
            My hot mama.

                   PATRICIA
        No. Say mon cherie.

                    MICHAEL
        Mon cherie. Mon cherie.

                   PATRICIA
Wait! Wait! What are you doing?! You
        didn't put the condom on.

                    MICHAEL
(he looks at the packet) Oh. That was a
    close call. (he sits up, freaked out
        that he almost made a baby)

PATRICIA
(she sits up) It's OK. Just be careful.

MICHAEL
This isn't working.

PATRICIA
I know. I'm sorry. I think we're just
trying to force something we're not
ready to do again.

MICHAEL
It's more than that. Us. Toi et moi.
This isn't working. Everything I do
just makes things worse. I don't know
what to do. I don't know how to make
you happy.

PATRICIA
You make me happy, Michael.

MICHAEL
No I don't. Not in the last couple of
weeks. You know that. I haven't treated
you like you deserve.

PATRICIA
I think we're just tired.

MICHAEL
No, it's me. Maybe I'm just not meant
to be in a relationship. I always seem
to screw it up. I don't know how to
act. I don't know what to do.

PATRICIA
We've had a lot on our minds.

MICHAEL
Even if I had plenty of rest and
nothing to think about I would find a
way to hurt you.

PATRICIA
Michael, you're the sweetest man I've
ever met. I love you.

MICHAEL
Let me help you with your dress. (he
buttons the back and kisses the back of
her neck) I love you. I'll walk you
out.

PATRICIA
You're sure? (Michael nods, Patricia
nods)

Michael walks Patricia down stairs and
gives her a kiss on the cheek. She
stays strong. He stands at the door and
watches her drive off. Michael assumes
Patricia will be fine with the break
up.

CUT TO:
EXTERIOR, PATRICIA'S HOME, SAME

CUT TO:
INTERIOR, 1963 CORVETTE, SAME

Parked at her house, Patricia breaks
down crying.

CUT TO:
INTERIOR, MICHELIN STORE, MORNING
Michael and Darnell are sitting in
Darnell's office.

DARNELL
So, that's it? You broke up with her?

MICHAEL
Yes. I can't make her happy and I don't
want to keep hurting her. I love her
too much.

DARNELL
Man, I'm sorry. I thought you two were
perfect for each other. I still do,
actually.

MICHAEL
Really?

DARNELL
Two people can be perfect for each
other and still have speed bumps in
their relationship. It's called life.
Getting past the challenges is what
strengthens your bond.

MICHAEL
Well, it doesn't matter. It's over.

                    DARNELL
I guess I can tell you now. Ginny and I
         had a pregnancy scare.

                    MICHAEL
                    Really?

                    DARNELL
   Mmm. Hmm. It was early in our
relationship. The first time we—. We
were young and dumb. Still had that
 young person's invincible mentality.
Ginny told me she was two months late.
I think she was more freaked out than I
was. So much so Ginny procrastinated in
   taking a pregnancy test. Then, she
didn't need to. It came a month later.
That was a month from hell. We argued a
  lot, cried a lot. We even bought a
                    crib.

                    MICHAEL
          You bought a crib!?

                    DARNELL
                  Sure did.

                    MICHAEL
Wow. There's a reality check for you.

                    DARNELL
I'd never been so happy to return an
                    item.

                    MICHAEL
                   I bet.

                     117

DARNELL
Life is about growing spiritually,
working off negative karma, learning,
helping others. That includes
forgiveness. Neither one of us did
anything wrong, but we were scared and
blamed each other for our distress.
When the false alarm passed, we
realized that we were being selfish and
promised to support each other through
anything and everything. You and
Patricia need to do the same. Put your
fear aside and trust that she will love
you no matter what.

MICHAEL
By now I'm sure she hates me no matter
what. Thanks for the pep talk, Darnell,
but it's too late. It's over. You're
stuck with me for eternity.

DARNELL
Forget that. I'm going to retire some
day. Sorry, but Ginny and I want to
travel. You're on your own. You'll have
to confide in a new manager.

MICHAEL
That almost makes me want to call
Patricia.

DARNELL
You should.

MICHAEL
I doubt she'd talk to me.

DARNELL
Give her some time. She'll forgive you.
Women just need time to cool off.
Patricia will miss you. Trust me.

MICHAEL
I would hope you're right, but. We
better get to work.

Michael and Darnell head to the front
of the store and Michael steps onto the
platform, begrudgingly, and becomes
inanimate. Darnell turns the CLOSED
sign to OPEN.

CUT TO:
INTERIOR, VICTORIAN HOME, DAY
Michael stands in front of his
bookcase. He shakes his head. One by
one Michael takes a
self-help/relationship book off of a
shelf, scans it, and places it in a
box.

MICHAEL
Where's advice on a pregnancy scare?
There should be a dating for dummies.
Yeah. Don't do it. Don't bother. Run
for the hills.

Michael grabs *Successful Dating at
Last!* He flips through it.

MICHAEL
"How do you feel about abortion? What
if it's *our* baby?" I don't know. I was
too scared to ask. We should have gone
through this book together. Oh, well.
Too late now.

Michael drops the book into the full
box and heads down stairs with the box
and places it outside by his door.

CUT TO:
EXTERIOR, VICTORIAN HOME, SAME

Neighbors 1, 2, and 3 walk by and look
at the several boxes of books by the
front door. There is a FREE sign on the
boxes.

NEIGHBOR NUMBER 1
Poor guy.

NEIGHBOR NUMBER 2
Poor guy.

NEIGHBOR NUMBER 3
You would think that at least one of
these books would have helped him.

NEIGHBOR NUMBER 2
They seemed so happy. I wonder what
happened.

NEIGHBOR NUMBER 1
Maybe too many books.

NEIGHBOR NUMBER 3
I've seen that on TV before. A woman
divorced her husband because he read
too much.

NEIGHBOR NUMBER 1
You would think that with a name like
Michael Mann his life would be cush.

NEIGHBOR NUMBER 3 (picks up book)
*Successful Dating at Last! A workbook
for understanding each other.* "What I
value in myself."

CUT TO:
INTERIOR, VICTORIAN HOME, SAME
Michael sits on the couch staring at
the TV. In the background the bookcase
is empty. Michael goes wide-eyed and
bolts downstairs and out of the house.

CUT TO:
EXTERIOR, VICTORIAN HOME, SAME
Michael grabs the workbook out of the
hands of Neighbor Number 3.

MICHAEL
I'll take that.

MICHAEL SULKS DURING THE SUMMER

CUT TO:
EXTERIOR, LIVRES, LATE AFTERNOON

Michael walks home from work and passes
Livres. Maryanne waves but he doesn't
notice.

CUT TO:
INTERIOR, LIVRES, SAME

MARYANNE
Ah. Poor guy. He was steps away from
freedom.

Michael passes Patricia's school.
Patricia is in the schoolyard saying
goodbye to the kids on their last day
of school. Parents are out front
waiting to receive their kids. Patricia
hugs each child, who fills with love
via Patricia's words.

LACY
Bye, Miss Leblanc. Thank you.

PATRICIA
Bye, Lacy. You're a beautiful person.
You come back and visit me anytime, OK.

PATRICIA (with another child)
You are smart and capable. Take care.

PATRICIA (with another child)
You are caring and you have a big
heart. I'll see you soon.

PATRICIA (with another child)
You are funny and a joy to have around.
Bye.

Patricia looks to the sidewalk and sees Michael walking by. He looks dazed and oblivious. She feels heartbroken, but puts back on a positive face and resumes seeing off her kids.

PARENT NUMBER 1 (to Michael)
Hey. Aren't you that director? Michael Mann.

LACY'S DAD
No. That's Miss Leblanc's boyfriend. Well, yes, that's Michael Mann, but not the director and not Miss Leblanc's boyfriend anymore.

Michael walks through the group of parents, tuned out to what anyone says. A few yards past, a 1963 Corvette, same color as Patricia's, drives by Michael and catches his eye. He brightens slightly and rubber necks hoping to see Patricia. It's not her. Michael resumes sulking.

CUT TO:
INTERIOR, VICTORIAN HOME, NIGHT
Michael sits on the edge of his bed and looks at pictures, on his phone, of himself with Patricia.

MICHAEL
"Time to cool off." Hmm. (Looks at
framed photo, on his night stand, of
Patricia) I don't deserve to have you
look at me like that anymore. (He puts
the frame face down. Michael puts his
right hand on his left shoulder to rub
it and moves his left elbow in circles
in the air) Breakup shoulder. Right on
time. How predictable. What does Louise
Hay say about aches? "Longing for love.
Longing to be held." Wise woman. (He
opens his nightstand drawer and takes
out pain pills.) No. That's the easy
way out.

Michael sits in the middle of the bed
and meditates.

CUT TO:
CHEVY DEALERSHIP, DAY
Michael walks by Chevy dealership. He
pauses and pans what would have all
been his, but now that he will
permanently be Michelin Mann he cannot
buy the dealership. Michael walks on.

CUT TO:
GOLDEN GATE BRIDGE, DAY
Michael stands at a railing along the
Golden Gate Bridge and looks out and
down.

                    MICHAEL
    If it weren't for the net . . . and
    Dolores Cannon. "What negative karma
     you don't work off in this lifetime
    you're going to have to come back and
    do it again with the same people, same
     circumstances, only worse next time."

                  KEVIN BRIGGS
    (cameo, "Guardian of the Golden Gate,"
              in civilian clothes)
             (walks up to Michael)
                   Hey there.

                    MICHAEL
    Oh. Hi. Uh. No, I'm not Michael Mann.

                     KEVIN
       Who's Michael Mann? How are you?

                    MICHAEL
            Not great. I feel alone.

                     KEVIN
             I'm sorry to hear that.

                    MICHAEL
    Thanks. How is that possible in a city
          of nearly a million people?

                     KEVIN
    What do you plan on doing tomorrow?

                    MICHAEL
    The usual. Work. Eat. Sleep. Have you
             ever thought about—

KEVIN
Jumping? Oh, sure. I know what it's
like to be in a dark place.

MICHAEL
So, why didn't you—

KEVIN
Jump?

MICHAEL
Before the net was here.

KEVIN
Suicide is frowned upon by (points
up) . . . I have to fulfill the
contract I came here with otherwise—

MICHAEL
You have to do it all over again.

KEVIN
Exactly.

MICHAEL
I'm just so confused. I thought things
were going well and I had things
figured out, but then—

KEVIN
Ask your Higher Self. You have all the
answers within you. You just have to
ask. Ask for a sign. In the meantime,
be gentle with yourself.

                    MICHAEL
    Even if there were no net (looking
    down), I'm sure I'd still survive.
                 Tires float.

                     KEVIN
                    Tires?

          MICHAEL (pats his stomach)
                 Spare tires.

                     KEVIN
    Ah. Well, it was nice talking with you.
                 See ya' round.

        MICHAEL (touches his stomach)
                 Ha. Good one.

                     KEVIN
    I'm Kevin Briggs by the way.

                    MICHAEL
    Michael Mann. (Kevin gives weird look:
    Michael said he wasn't Michael Mann)
    Nice to meet you. And thanks. (Kevin
    walks off) The contract. Right. Am I
    sure I signed it? (laughs) Were there
       witnesses? Does Heaven have copy
       machines or are they still using
    carbon? (laughs) Was my contract carbon
       dated? Ha. I should have been a
          comedian. I already have the
    credentials: depression with suicidal
                   thoughts.

CUT TO:
INTERIOR, VICTORIAN HOME, NIGHT
Michael lies in bed looking up at the
ceiling.

MICHAEL
Higher Self, please show me a sign. Am
I really doomed to be Michelin Man
forever? Thanks for sending Kevin my
way. Cool dude.

CUT TO:
INTERIOR, MICHELIN STORE, MORNING

Michael goes to step onto the platform
to become Michelin Man and he trips on
the step. He turns wide-eyed toward
Darnell, who is walking past to turn
the CLOSED sign to OPEN.

MICHAEL
Did you see that?

DARNELL
I sure did. Wow!

MICHAEL
That's the first time I've ever tripped
on the step.

DARNELL
I've never seen you trip on the step
before.

                    MICHAEL
              Wow. That's a sign.

                    DARNELL
     The universe gives us signs every day.
        I'm glad you're taking notice.

                    MICHAEL
     Do you think maybe there's a chance—

                    DARNELL
            You have all the answers.

               MICHAEL (looks up)
     Thank you. I could sure use an angel,
                     too.

     Michael hesitatingly steps onto the
       platform and becomes Michelin Man.
     Darnell turns the CLOSED sign to OPEN,
       looks back at Michael, and sees that
     Michael is Michelin Man again. Darnell
       walks up to Michelin Man and puts his
         hand on Michelin Man's shoulder.

                    DARNELL
                 Fight for it.

           7 1/2 HOURS LATER

     Teal Swan (cameo) walks into the store.
       Michael goes wide-eyed, because he
                recognizes her.

                    TEAL (to Darnell)
        Hi. I was just passing through the area
          and one of my tires went flat.

                       DARNELL
        You came to the right place. I'd be
        happy to help. (leans to look outside)
              Is that yours? The tour bus?

                        TEAL
                        Yes.

                       DARNELL
                  Rock star, huh?

                        TEAL
        I like to think so. I'm grateful the
         flat happened when it did. It would
        have been awful to have been stuck on
              the Golden Gate Bridge.

                       DARNELL
        Everything happens for a reason. Sorry.
        I didn't mean to impose my beliefs on
        you. You probably don't believe in all
          that hoodoo guru nonsense anyway.

                        TEAL
                You'd be surprised.

                       DARNELL
        Have a seat. I'll have one of my guys
        pull the bus in and get you situated.

                        TEAL
                    Thank you.

                         130

Darnell walks into the shop (garage depots). Teal walks up to Michelin Man and stands squarely to him. Michelin Man goes wide-eyed and Teal notices. She can see him for who he really is, which surprises her. Teal wasn't expecting him to be human.

                    TEAL
Oh. (long pause as she reads him) Mine (her books thrown out), too? She's a beautiful woman. I can see why your souls aligned. You'll get her back. To fight for her you have to fight for yourself—demand to understand the core of your being. That takes courage. Well, you were almost at the core but you stopped searching too soon. Fear stops most people from going all the way. Removing mental blocks can help you ride smoothly for a while, but if you don't understand the core of your being you'll hit another speed bump. Watch my video on core imprints. (Michael winks) You're welcome.

DARNELL (walks back into shop, Teal is
                  seated)
OK, Miss. Your bus is ready to get back on the road.

                    TEAL
Thank you. (long pause, she reads him) Have you picked out a name, yet?

                    131

DARNELL
A name for what?

TEAL
Oh, (looks at name tag) Darnell. Thanks
for everything, Darnell.

DARNELL
You're welcome.

Teal walks out of the store and Darnell
follows her to the door to turn the
OPEN sign to CLOSED. Michael bounces
off the platform.

MICHAEL
That was Teal Swan!

Michael runs out the door, but somehow
a huge tour bus disappeared into thin
air.

CUT TO:
EXTERIOR, MICHELIN STORE, SAME,
LATE AFTERNOON

Michael looks around. Teal is gone.
Then, he notices a white feather on the
ground. It is a swan feather, which
looks like an angel's wing.

CUT TO:
INTERIOR, MICHELIN STORE, SAME

                    DARNELL
            What was that all about?

                    MICHAEL
      That was Teal Swan. She's a spiritual
      teacher. I read all of her books. And
            threw out all of her books.

                    DARNELL
            So, she's not a rock star?

                    MICHAEL
               She is to me.

                  CUT TO:
      INTERIOR, VICTORIAN HOME, SAME,
                  EVENING

      Michael stands in front of his nearly
               empty bookcase.
      MICHAEL (as though talking to Teal)
                  Sorry.

      Michael sits at the dining table with
      his laptop, pen, and paper. He loads
         Teal's video on core imprints.
            MICHAEL (to himself)
      What's this about core imprints?

TEAL

*"Before we come into this life, we set
an intention for the life that we
intend to experience. That intention
sets in motion the entire chain of
events leading to this specific life
itself. This core experience is the
root from which everything will grow.
We always choose this core experience
before birth. The feeling signature of
the 'opposite' of your ultimate desire
for this life becomes your core
imprint. It is the thing you came into
this life to transform. It is your main
purpose for life to use the contrast of
that particular feeling signature to
find and become it's [sic] opposite."
[From Teals Swan's YouTube channel]*

MICHAEL
I know what my main purpose for life
is. That's easy. To be a mobilizer. (He
writes "mobilizer" and other notes) So,
what would be the opposite of
mobilizer? Mobilizer. Mobile. Immobile.
Immobilizer. Immobile. What does
immobile have to do with me? (He
pictures himself as Michelin Man) Oh. I
am immobile. How do I mobilize people
if I'm immobile? I guess I have to
experience immobile to have awareness
and experience of mobile. But I don't
want to be immobile forever. I've been
so scared of being immobile forever
that I've blocked myself from
mobilizing my heart and moving forward
in life with someone. That's it!

Michael bolts downstairs and out the
door.

CUT TO:
EXTERIOR, VICTORIAN HOME, SAME
Michael runs across the street to Alamo
Square Park.

MICHAEL (yells toward Patricia's house)
Patricia! Patricia! Patricia, I'm
sorry!

Lights in the neighborhood turn on.
Neighbors 1, 2, and 3 look out their
windows and at each other.

135

Michael runs back into his house.

CUT TO:
INTERIOR, VICTORIAN HOME, SAME
Michael runs upstairs and sits on the
edge of his bed and calls Patricia. He
gets her voicemail.

PATRICIA
*Hi, You reached Patricia. I'll call you
back as soon as I get a chance. Bye.*

MICHAEL
—Patricia, it's me Michael.
—I'm sorry.
—I need to talk to you.
—I'm a mobilizer.
—I'm a mobilizer.
—I know I'm not making any sense.
—I want to move forward with you.
—I need to talk to you.
—OK.
—Bye.

Michael sits on his bed and thinks and
then he calls Darnell and gets his
voicemail.

DARNELL
*Hey, what's up. It's Darnell. You know
what to do.*

                    MICHAEL
            —Darnell, it's Michael.
    —Call me as soon as you get this.
            —I need to talk to you.
        —It can't wait 'til morning.
                    —OK.
                    —Bye.
    Michael calls Maryanne and gets her
            voicemail at the store.

                    MARYANNE
    Bonjour and merci for calling Livres.
    Sorry we missed your call. We're open
    daily from 8 a.m. to 6 p.m. We'll call
    you back as soon as we hear your
            message. Au revoir.

                    MICHAEL
    —Maryanne, it's Michael, Patricia's
                boyfr—Well.
    —I was—I—if she'll—please call me back.
                —Thanks.
                    —Bye.

                    CUT TO:
    EXTERIOR, DARNELL'S HOME, SAME,
                    NIGHT
    Michael knocks feverishly on Darnell's
    home front door. Michael looks like he
    just ran a marathon. The house goes
    from dark to one light on. Darnell
            answers the door.

                    137

DARNELL
Michael. What are you doing here? Do
you know what time it is? What happened
to you?

MICHAEL
Sorry. I really need to talk to you. I
know it's late. Can I come in?

CUT TO:
INTERIOR, DARNELL'S HOME, SAME

MICHAEL
I—

DARNELL
Shh. Keep it down.

MICHAEL
I'm sorry.

DARNELL
It's OK. We were up. Ginny's not
feeling well. Some intestinal
infection. What are you doing?

MICHAEL
Darnell, I had to tell you. I am a
mobilizer. I'm meant to mobilize
people.

DARNELL
Yes. You sell tires. That's one way of
looking at it.

MICHAEL
No. I've been so scared of being
immobile forever that I've blocked
myself from mobilizing my heart and
moving forward in life with someone.
How can I mobilize people the way I
really want to if I'm forever immobile?
I have to face my fear and move forward
with Patricia. I don't know if I can
have kids or if they'll have to live
the same life I have, but I'm willing
to take a chance.

Darnell walks into his home office and
kneels at the safe. He is about to turn
the combination lock and then he looks
back and sees Michael in the doorway.
Darnell gives Michael a do-you-mind
look.

MICHAEL
I'll just wait out here.

Darnell takes out a very old book
dating back to the late 1800s, shuts
the safe, meets Michael in the living
room, sits next to Michael on the
couch, and puts the book on the coffee
table.

DARNELL
I guess you're ready to see this.

MICHAEL
Whoa. What is that?

DARNELL

It's Michelin's manifesto. Covenant.
Articles of Incorporation. I call it
Michelin's Bible. It's been passed down
through generations of Michelin
managers since the Michelin brothers
started their business in 1889.

MICHAEL
How did you get a hold of it?

DARNELL
I have my ways.

MICHAEL
Manager of the year? (They laugh) Why
isn't it still in France where the
company started?

DARNELL
Do you want me to show it to you or
not?

MICHAEL
Yes. Is there something about love?

DARNELL
Well, you already know that you were
given three chances at finding the
right girl or you would be inanimate
forever.

MICHAEL
Yes.

                    DARNELL
        Well, listen to this: (reads) If
        Michelin Man experiences true love,
         then he will not only be animate
        forever but also live a life like any
        human, including but not limited to,
          aging, emoting, and procreating.

                    MICHAEL
        I CAN have children! But, will they—

                    DARNELL
        Hold on there, Dr. Masters, there's
        more. (reads) Michelin Man's offspring
        will be immediately and permanently
        animate as to immortalize Monsieur
             Rossillon's creation.

                MICHAEL (stands)
        I can be a father! A grandfather!

                    DARNELL
                     Shh!

                    MICHAEL
        Oh, this is good news. I have to get to
                    Patricia.

                    DARNELL
          Go get her, Victor Hugo.

                    MICHAEL
        Thank you thank you, Darnell.

        Michael leans in to give Darnell a hug
                   and kiss.

                      141

                    DARNELL (puts his hand up)
                    Not necessary.

                    MICHAEL
              I'll see you tomorrow.

                    DARNELL
                    Or, not.

Michael runs out the door.

                   CUT TO:
          EXTERIOR, LIVRES, MORNING,
                   7:30 a.m.
Michael runs up to Livres and reads the
             sign on the door:
       LIVRES IS OUT OF BUSINESS. OWNER
RETIRED. THANK YOU FOR YOUR BUSINESS.
            YOU WILL BE MISSED.

                    MICHAEL
Out of business? Retired? But— I— She
     really went through with it.

Michael collapses to the ground and
sits slumped over against Maryanne's
door at Livres. He falls asleep.

                   CUT TO:
     EXTERIOR, LIVRES, SAME, 8:30 a.m.
   Maryanne walks up to Livres and sees
   Michael asleep against her door, but
   doesn't realize at first that it's him.

MARYANNE (to herself)
Oh, no. Not again. Poor guy. This city really needs to take care of the homeless.
(to Michael)
Hi. Hey, buddy. Excuse me. Sorry to wake you. I need to get in my store. Here's $5.00. Why don't you get a coffee and something to eat?

MICHAEL
Maryanne!

MARYANNE
Michael?!

MICHAEL
Maryanne, I've been trying to get a hold of you. I need to talk to you. I need to talk to Patricia. I can't find her. I—

MARYANNE
Slow down. Get up. Come on in. I'll get you some water.

CUT TO:
INTERIOR, LIVRES, SAME

MARYANNE
Sit down. What happened to you?

143

MICHAEL

I need to talk to Patricia. I realized
that I had to be immobile in order to
have awareness of and to experience
being mobile and mobilizing others. I
don't have to be afraid of being
immobile forever, anymore.

MARYANNE
That's right dear.

MICHAEL

I've been so scared of being immobile
forever that I've blocked myself from
mobilizing my heart and moving forward
in life with someone. That someone is
Patricia. I need to find her.

MARYANNE

It makes me so happy to hear you say
that. I was hoping you'd get there. You
two are perfect for each other.

MICHAEL

And I talked to Darnell. He showed me
Michelin's . . . uh . . . what's it
called . . . the—

MARYANNE
I call it Michelin's Bible.

MICHAEL
Right. That's what Darnell calls it. It
says that I can have children and that
they will be animate permanently from
the start. Wait. How did you know about
Michelin's Bible?

MARYANNE
I've been waiting a long time to tell
you. My great grandfather, on my
mother's side, was Marius Rossillon,
the creator of Bibendum.

MICHAEL
You're a descendant of Monsieur
Rossillon—the man who created me?

MARYANNE
Oui.

MICHAEL
Wow. So, then Patricia and I are
related. Kind of. We can't—

MARYANNE
Quite the opposite. Marius knew only
one of his descendants could unlock
your heart. And Patricia's the one
with—

MICHAEL
The key! Patricia. I have to find her.
Do you know where she is? I've been
looking and calling all night.

MARYANNE
She's gone. It's OK, though. She's just
in New York.

MICHAEL
New York?!

MARYANNE
I guess you didn't hear. She took the
job. I'm sorry, dear. I thought you
knew.

MICHAEL
But, it's not even September, yet. She
said that the job started after Labor
Day.

MARYANNE
She had to go a week early for
training. Oh, Michael, I'm sorry. I'm
sure you can figure out something. I'll
talk to her for you.

MICHAEL
She's gone. She knows. I'd move to New
York, too, if I knew I was in a
relationship with a stack of tires.

MARYANNE
Oh, no, Michael. She doesn't know.

MICHAEL
Really?

MARYANNE
No, I never let on. Patricia was
devastated when you broke up with her.
She really loved you. I guess since you
two couldn't work things out, and I was
planning on retiring and traveling, she
had nothing left to tie her to San
Francisco.

MICHAEL
She doesn't know. I have to tell her.
(looks at his watch) I need to get to
work. If you talk with Patricia could
you please tell her I love her and I
want to talk to her?

MARYANNE
Of course.

MICHAEL
Thanks, Maryanne, (gives her kiss on
the cheek) for everything.

MARYANNE
You're welcome.

CUT TO:
EXTERIOR, LIVRES, SAME

Michael bolts out the door and runs to
Michelin Store, so that he will be on
time.

147

CUT TO:
INTERIOR, MICHELIN STORE, SAME,
8:50 a.m.

Patricia walks into the store a few minutes before it opens. She makes eye contact with Darnell, whose eyes go wide and then he immediately tries to look busy and goes into his office.

PATRICIA
Hello? Hello!

Patricia walks over to Darnell's office and knocks on the opened door.

PATRICIA
Hi, Darnell. Is Michael in, yet?

DARNELL
Uh, hi. No. Not yet.

PATRICIA
Do you know what time he's supposed to be here?

DARNELL
I don't know.

PATRICIA
I really need to talk to him. It's important.

DARNELL (looking down at his desk)
Mmm hmm.

PATRICIA
Darnell, You and I don't know each
other very well, but Michael talks so
much about you. I feel like I know you.
You're his best friend.

DARNELL
Michael and I go way back.

PATRICIA
I really need to talk to him. Please. I
thought I was—

DARNELL (still looking down)
I know.

PATRICIA
You do?

DARNELL (looks up)
Yes. Michael told me. Before he broke
broke up with you. He's been trying to
find you, you know.

PATRICIA
I know. I know. I've been avoiding him.
I know it's wrong, but he's just so
secretive. He's hiding something, and I
don't know what it is. I'm scared.

DARNELL

Have a seat. (Patricia sits) When our company was started in the late 1800s, the cartoonist who designed our logo was a Merlin of sorts. Legend has it, the artist cast a spell on his creation, which he wanted to be immortal. If the company could last 100 years, then Michelin Man—Michael to you—could have the opportunity to become human and reproduce and have his offspring reproduce and so on and so on, making the artist's creation immortal. In order to become human permanently, Michelin Man would have to find everlasting love. You see, the cartoonist was French.

PATRICIA
Ah.

DARNELL
The French are the quintessential romantics.

PATRICIA
So, how does it work?

DARNELL

After our company hit the 100-year mark
in 1989, Michelin Man started taking
human form after store hours. Michelin
Man, Michael, still has to work his day
job, in pose as our mascot, but after
hours he's human. For the last couple
years, he's been seeking love, bon
vivant, and eternal "life."

PATRICIA

That explains why he could never get
together with me during the work day.
He always said he was too busy. But he
never talked about work. I never knew
what he did here. I thought maybe he
was a spy. This was his cover.

DARNELL

There's one other thing you need to
know. Legend also has it that Michelin
Man has only three chances at finding
true love. You're number three. After
the third strike, he's doomed to be
inanimate forever.

PATRICIA

Even after hours?!

DARNELL

Even after hours. You really care about
him don't you?

PATRICIA

Yeah. Yeah, I do. I love him. I
just . . . I didn't . . .

Michael walks in and sees Patricia and
is conflicted, because he's excited to
see her, but is still afraid for her to
see him become Michelin Man in the
upcoming minutes. He turns to walk out,
but can't because Joanne is about to
walk in. He has to avoid both. Joanne
wants to get back together. How did
Joanne figure out where he worked? See
name badge? Paycheck? Darnell sees
what's happening. Michael turns back
toward the store and takes his place in
the mascot position. He's not really
inanimate, though, because it's not
9 a.m. yet.

DARNELL
(jumps out of his chair and closes the
blinds in his office.)
I'll give you a little privacy. Excuse
me while I help another customer. (He
closes door, under his breath) Here we
go.

Joanne walks in.
DARNELL
Can I help you?

JOANNE
Yeah. Is Michael here?

DARNELL
No. I, uh, gave him the day off.

Darnell sees REBECCA walk into the
store.
Is Michael here?

DARNELL
No. He won't be in 'til later.

JOANNE
I thought he had the day off.

REBECCA (to Joanne)
Who are you?

JOANNE
Who are you?

In the background Michael looks back
and forth like he's watching a tennis
match. He is worried, but is happy to
see two women fighting over him.

REBECCA
I'm Rebecca. I'm Michael's . . . well,
we're not together, but we used to be.
He wants to be. I want us to get back
together.

JOANNE
Michael wants to be together with *me*.
We're going to get back together.
Michael shakes his head. REBECCA and
JOANNE look back at him and then at
Darnell. (they motion toward Michael)
Did he just move?

Darnell is about to say something, and
Patricia walks out of the office.
Michael mouths *oh no*.

PATRICIA
What's going on out here?

DARNELL
These ladies were just leaving.

REBECCA and JOANNE
Leaving?!

REBECCA (to Patricia)
Who are you?

PATRICIA (to Rebecca)
Who are you?

JOANNE (to Patricia)
Yeah. Who are you?

PATRICIA (to both)
I'm Michael's girlfriend. Who are you?

Rebecca and Joanne walk over to Michael
and stand against him at his sides and
touch his face. They look toward
Darnell and Patricia. Michael gives a
sly smile. Patricia sneers. Michael
mouths *sorry* to Patricia.

REBECCA
We used to be in a relationship with
Michael and one of us is going to get
back together with him.

154

PATRICIA
Over my dead body.

DARNELL
That's my cue. (He walks back to
office)

The ground starts rumbling and
everything in the store shakes. Joanne
and Rebecca scream and run out of the
store. Michael jumps on Patricia to
protect her, they fall to the ground,
and a chandelier falls, narrowly
missing them. The ground stops shaking.
They brush themselves off.

MICHAEL
Are you OK?

PATRICIA
Yes. Yes, I think so. I'm sorry. I—

MICHAEL
No, I'm sorry. You see the thing is—

PATRICIA
I know.

MICHAEL
You do?

PATRICIA
Yes. I talked to Darnell. He told me
everything.

MICHAEL
I'm sorry. I should have told you. I
was just so afraid of losing you. I
thought that if you knew, you wouldn't
want to be with me. I love you. I don't
want to lose you. I want to spend the
rest of my life with you.

PATRICIA
I love you, too. It's OK. Everyone has
quirks. Everyone is inanimate every
once in a while. It's called vegging
out.

They laugh. At 8:59 a.m. Patricia and
Michael kiss. While they're still
kissing, the clock strikes 9 a.m., and
they stop kissing. Their eyes go wide,
wondering if Michael will turn
inanimate. He doesn't. They're
relieved. They embrace and continue
kissing. The clock striking nine and
Michael still being human solidifies
their true and everlasting love. While
Patricia and Michael are still kissing,
Darnell takes a cardboard cutout of
Michelin Man out of his office and
places it where Michael used to stand.

DARNELL
I've been looking forward to this day.

Michael and Patricia continue kissing
and Darnell walks to front door to turn
the CLOSED sign to OPEN. He looks back
to Michael and Patricia still in an
embrace on the floor, kissing, and
decides to keep the store closed. He
locks the door and walks back to his
office.

Credits Roll

THE END

FLIGHT PATTERN

FADE IN:
EXT. CIA HEADQUARTERS—DAY

CUT TO:
INT. CIA HEADQUARTERS
See people walk back and forth through
the lobby as camera pans the large CIA
logo on the floor. Can only see people
from the waist down. One person roller
skates through, moon walking. There are
two broomball (actual brooms) players.
A dog chases a cat. A blind man is
tripped.

CUT TO:
INTERROGATION ROOM IN CIA
HEADQUARTERS
CIA agents Hugh Saine and Ann Byn-
Ladden look through a one-way mirror
into a room where an Asian Man sits in
a chair, tied up. He clearly has been
tortured and interrogated for hours.
Nothing is working, and almost
everything has been tried.

HUGH
(to Ann)
Ann, he still won't talk. You know what
we need to do, don't you?

159

ANN
Yeah. American music. They hate
American music. It works every time,
Hugh.

Ann scrolls through her phone's
playlists: Caught the bad guy, Bad guy
talked, Get pumped, Workout,
Interrogation. She clicks on
Interrogation and sees the artists:
Taylor Swift, Garth Brooks, Kanye West,
Alanis Morisette, Milli Vanilli,
Britney Spears, Miley Cyrus, Lady Gaga,
Justin Bieber, The Cranberries. She
clicks on The Cranberries and plays
"Zombie" on repeat through the room's
speaker system, and then the two agents
walk away. Five hours later, the agents
look through the one-way mirror and
find that the song is stuck on the word
Zombie, and Asian Man is hitting the
back of his head against the chair
trying to kill himself. The agents stop
the music and enter the room.

HUGH
Now will you talk?

Asian Man shakes his head.
ANN
The big Dubrowski isn't going to be
happy. Here he comes.

CIA boss Jeff Dubrowski enters room.

                    JEFF DUBROWSKI
                  (to Ann and Hugh)
          Agents Saine and Byn-Ladden, did he
            tell you what we need to know?

                    HUGH AND ANN
                      No, Sir.

                       JEFF
          Then we have only one option left. Book
           him on a Uniting Air flight. Keep him
          here overnight and leave first thing in
                    the morning.

                    HUGH AND ANN
                     Yes, Sir.

             Jeff leaves the room.

          As the agents leave the room . . .
                       ANN
                  (to Asian Man)
               You had your chance.

                     DAY 2
          EXT. DULLES AIRPORT—MORNING
          Full police escort drives up to
        departures area with Hugh and Ann in
         the backseat of one car, sitting on
      either side of handcuffed (in front of
      body) and shackled Asian Man. The cars
          stop, and Hugh and Ann (wearing
       backpacks) and Asian Man walk toward
                    security.

                        HUGH
                      (to Ann)
        If he doesn't talk by the time we get
        to Honolulu, then we won't have to go
            much farther to deport him.

                        ANN
        I'm looking forward to Hawaii. I need a
                     vacation.

                        HUGH
                      Me, too.

                     ASIAN MAN
              We go to Hawaii!? Cool.

                        ANN
        Don't get too excited. You've obviously
        never flown on Uniting Air. We may
            never make it to Honolulu.

                      CUT TO:
                  DULLES SECURITY
        Hugh and Ann walk through x-ray machine
        without stopping and then Asian Man is
        waved in by male, Dulles TSA agent Jack
                       Carson.

                        JACK
               Put your arms up.

        Asian Man gives him a look like, are
        you mental? Asian Man can't move his
                  shackled arms.

                        162

                    JACK
                 My bad.

2D image of Asian Man is lit up with
   errors. Asian Man is sent out and
   female, Dulles TSA agent Rita Ford
takes off his dress belt. He's x-rayed
again; with errors showing Asian Man is
sent out to take off his shoes. He's x-
rayed again; with errors showing Asian
   Man is sent out to take off his
   glasses. Five minutes later, he's in
   the machine again wearing only his
undies, still shackled. Still, the 2D
      image shows a problem.

An hour later, Asian Man is in an
office with Hugh, Ann, Jack, and Rita.
Jack and Rita are using wands to figure
out where the metal is. They realize
   that it's the handcuffs and shackles
   that are setting off x-ray machine.

                    JACK
                 (to Rita)
             It's the shackles.
          (to Hugh, Ann, Asian Man)
      Alright. You're free to leave.
             (to Hugh and Ann)
Oh, by the way. Agents Hugh Saine, Ann
               Byn-Ladden.

                HUGH AND ANN
                   Yeah.

                    163

                    JACK
          Hugh Saine, Ann Byn-Ladden?

                  HUGH AND ANN
                      Yeah?

                    JACK
                  Never mind.

    The last to arrive at the gate, Hugh,
      Ann, and Asian Man are bumped.

          Dulles Gate Agent KRISTI
              (to Hugh and Ann)
          Hugh Saine, Ann Byn-Ladden?

                  HUGH AND ANN
                      Yes.

      KRISTI with worried, puzzled look on
                  her face . . .
          Hugh Saine, Ann Byn-Ladden.

                    ANN
          What? Is something wrong?

                   KRISTI
    Oh, no. No. Uh. No. It, uh, seems this
    flight is, uh, overbooked. We're going
    to have to put you on the next flight.

                    HUGH
    Oh, no worries. We're in no hurry. (He
    takes new boarding passes.) Thanks.

    Asian Man rolls his eyes impatiently.

                     164

Hugh, Ann, and Asian Man stay at that
gate for the next flight. While
waiting, people all around them talk
loudly on the phone. Each person plugs
one ear and stares down someone else
for talking loudly on the phone. (Do
you mind?! attitude)

The gate's estimated departure time
display changes to one hour late . . .
two hours late . . . three hours late.
Hugh and Ann look at their watches.

                    ANN
                  (to Hugh)
You know what this means, don't you? We
    might miss our connecting flight in
                  O'Hare.

Asian Man rolls his eyes impatiently.

                    HUGH
Oh, well. The more time I spend in an
airport, the more of an excuse I have
            to eat junk food.

                    ANN
    If you're not careful there, your
belly's going to get to O'Hare before
                  you do.

Hugh inspects his pudgy belly.

                ASIAN MAN
        You American all alike.

165

                    CUT TO:
            CHICAGO SKYLINE, NIGHT

                    CUT TO:
                 INT. O'HARE
Hugh, Ann, and Asian Man rush to the
gate of the next flight. On the way,
Ann looks at her wrist pedometer that
is racking up steps and ticking away
like an old tally counter. The numbers
are rolling fast. On a moving walkway,
Hugh and Ann stand on either side of
Asian Man holding onto him. Right
before the end of the walkway, Hugh and
Ann let go of him and walk off and keep
walking, thinking he's still with them.
Asian Man trips at the end and falls
        face first. They look back.

                HUGH AND ANN
                   Oops.

They walk back and help him up. Asian
Man gives them the stink eye. They
finally make it to their gate. The
clock ticks to 10 minutes before
departure. O'Hare, male gate agent
Cammy closes door. Hugh, Ann, and Asian
        Man are panting.

                   HUGH
                (to Cammy)
                 We made it!

CAMMY
I'm sorry, Sir. The door must be closed
exactly 10 minutes before departure.

HUGH
But we're here. We made it in time!

CAMMY
Thirty seconds ago would have been in
time. Now, you're late.

ANN
(flashes her badge)
Sir. What's your name? Cammy? Cammy,
we're CIA agents transporting a
criminal. You have to let us on.

CAMMY
Oh, Agents Hugh Saine, Ann Byn-Ladden?

ANN
Yes. So, you'll let us on?

CAMMY
Oh, no. Former president of Iraq and
founder of al-Qaeda?

HUGH
I don't know what you're talking about.

CAMMY

Where's Agent Orange? Let me guess, the
gate for Vietnam? I don't care if
you're the Dalai Lama or a Peruvian
llama. You're not getting on this
flight or any other tonight. This is
the last one out. Have a good evening.

Asian Man rolls his eyes.

ANN

You haven't heard the last of me.

CAMMY

Nope. See you in the morning.

Hugh, Ann, and Asian Man settle into
seats at that gate, knowing that they
will spend the night there and assuming
their morning flight will be from that
gate.

DAY 3

Midnight, CST

Hugh and Ann were annoyed with Cammy,
but otherwise aren't annoyed with
delays. They're getting paid. They stay
awake all night. They sit on either
side of Asian Man. They load a movie on
one's phone and put it in front of
Asian Man, so that both agents can see
the screen. The movie is *Bridget
Jones's Diary*.

ASIAN MAN
Ugh! Renée Zellweger!

HUGH AND ANN
Shut up!

1 a.m., CST
Asian Man is trying to sleep, but
can't.

Heard overhead:
"The walkway is ending. Please, watch
your step."
"The walkway is ending. Please, watch
your step."
"The walkway is ending. Please, watch
your step."
"The walkway is ending. Please, watch
your step."
"The walkway is ending. Please, watch
your step."
"The walkway is ending. Please, watch
your step."
"The walkway is ending. Please, watch
your step."

Asian Man bangs his head against the
back of the chair to try to kill
himself. Hugh and Ann relax and share
ear buds to listen to movie on phone.

2 a.m., CST
Passenger cart goes back and forth
beeping and red light spinning and
flashing.

3 a.m., CST
Someone vacuums and hits Asian Man's feet. Hugh and Ann pick up their feet.

4 a.m., CST
Someone walks with floor polisher.

5 a.m., CST
Outside, garbage truck beeps and garbage bin makes crashing sound.

6 a.m., CST
Someone walks with leaf blower (by Hugh, Ann, and Asian Man).

7 a.m., CST
It's finally quiet. Asian Man is just about to doze off and Hugh and Ann wake him.

HUGH AND ANN
Let's go.

They think that they are about to board the 7:25 a.m., CST, flight to San Jose at the gate where they're sitting, but they check the monitor and find that the flight will leave from a different gate. They rush. Ann's pedometer is rolling, again. It takes them 15 minutes to get to the right gate and arrive just in time.

Cammy collects tickets from Hugh and Ann.

                    CAMMY
      Oh, I see the important people are
                     back.

                     ANN
               Good morning.

They board, and the flight leaves at
7:55 a.m., CST, and is due to arrive in
     San Jose at 10:30 a.m., PST

                  CUT TO:
                   CABIN
        Hugh looks at his watch:
              10:00 a.m. PST.

                    HUGH
                  (to Ann)
We should have started our descent by
                     now.

                     ANN
      I know. I wonder what's going on.

                    HUGH
Something's wrong. (He looks out his
    window.) We're over the Pacific.

                     ANN
              How can that be?

CUT TO:
INT. COCKPIT
Pilot Phillips, First Officer Schmidt,
and Navigator Columbus are swiveled in
their chairs facing each other and the
center of the cockpit, leaning forward
with their forearms on their thighs,
playing with their phones. Columbus
does a double take at his instrument
panel.

COLUMBUS
Schmidt! We're off course!! Captain
Phillips! We overshot the airport.

Captain Phillips, Schmidt, and Columbus
quickly put their phones away and
resume flying positions.

CUT TO:
CABIN

CAPTAIN PHILLIPS
(on public address system [PA])
Ladies and Gentlemen, this is your
captain speaking. Some of you may have
noticed, by now, that we are over the
Pacific. We seemed to have overshot the
San Jose Airport by 150 miles. No need
to be alarmed. Just . . . technical
difficulties. Nothing to see here.
We're going to turn back now. Sorry for
the inconvenience. We'll get you on the
ground as soon as possible.

ANN
(to Hugh)
Do you think we'll make our next
flight?

Asian Man rolls his eyes.

HUGH
It would have been nice if the pilot
had just kept going west to Honolulu.
Oh, well. I'm in no hurry.

Asian Man hits his head against the
seat.

FADE IN:
EXT. SAN JOSE AIRPORT—DAY, MID-
MORNING
A long shot of the airport with planes
taking off and landing. Then, zoom in
on man driving full luggage cart to
plane. He whips the cart just as he
stops suddenly at the plane. One
suitcase falls off. He looks back and
notices and shrugs it off. After the
other luggage is put on the plane, he
whips his cart around and drives off,
running over the stranded suitcase. He
looks back and shrugs, again. Then,
another worker walks by it and ignores
it. Then, a third worker walks by and
checks the tag, but leaves the bag
there. Then, the garbage man comes by
and throws it in the back of his truck.

CUT TO:

EXT. FRONT OF SAN JOSE AIRPORT— DAY, MID-MORNING

The unloading zone. Married couple Lisa and Harold are hugging and kissing goodbye with their eyes closed. Lisa feels like she's being watched. She opens one eye and sees male, Black, parking cop (wearing only one white, glittery glove—on right hand) standing behind her husband.

LISA
(to Parking Cop)
Do you mind?

PARKING COP
"Excuse me. You're standing still in a no-parking zone. If you don't get a move on that body, [I mean car], I'll be forced to give you a ticket." [from Midnight Star's song "No Parking on the Dance Floor"]

Lisa gives Parking Cop a weird look.

LOUDSPEAKER
Midnight Star's song plays. "No
parking, baby. No parking on the dance
floor. Beep Beep." The song continues
to play. Parking Cop dances. The low-
rider car with hopping suspension
behind Lisa's car beeps twice with
song. Lisa and Harold wave goodbye as
Harold dances into the terminal. Song
continues to play as Lisa drives off.

Harold stares blankly at the check-in
kiosk. Ticket Agent Allison walks up.

                HAROLD
            (to Allison)
        Can you please help me?

                ALLISON
    Oh, no. I'm not authorized. You can
            figure it out.

                HAROLD
    If I have to learn another computer
    program, it's going to be one that
    earns me money, not takes my money.
    Allison walks away and Harold figures
it out. He then walks up to Allison and
        puts his bag on the scale.

                ALLISON
            Here's your tag.

                HAROLD
        Can't you put it on for me?

                    ALLISON
          Oh, no. I'm not authorized.

                    HAROLD
     What exactly are you authorized to do?

                    ALLISON
     Your bag is over the allowable weight.

     Harold takes out his 2 ½-year-old
     child, Jimmy, he was trying not to pay
                     for.

                    HAROLD
       I'm going to need another ticket.

     The ticket agent reserves a seat and
     throws the bag on the conveyor belt.
     The bag has a crumpled tag that Harold
     couldn't fold properly. Then, Allison
       eyes a tip jar on the counter.

                    HAROLD
      I'm not going to give you any more
                    money!

     As Harold and Jimmy walk away from the
     counter, they see Morbidly Obese Woman
       standing on another luggage scale.

CUT TO:
SECURITY CHECKPOINT
Teri is in x-ray machine with her shirt
up, exposing her belly unnecessarily
and moving sexy. TSA Agent Rodney Kline
drools, googly eyes.

RODNEY
You look good.

He waves her through.

TERI
I know.

RODNEY
Uh, uh, I mean . . .

Harold, worried about his son's
exposure to radiation, throws his son
through x-ray machine to Rodney.

ROBERTA
(wears scarf on head, newly diagnosed
with cancer)
(to Rodney)
Do the stewardesses on my flight serve
chemotherapy?

RODNEY
Yes, but they don't take
insurance . . . and they require exact
change.

Roberta walks through x-ray machine, back and forth *many* times, using it as radiation therapy.

ROBERTA
I'm cured!

Marie is about to walk through x-ray machine toward TSA Agent Renee McAllister.

RENEE
(to Marie)
What's this? (Motion's to own waist)

Marie is wearing yoga pants with extra material that goes around the hips. She tilts her head as she examines Renee's waist.

MARIE
Excess belly fat?

RENEE
No. You.

MARIE
It's just part of the pants.

Renee allows Marie into then out of the x-ray machine. Renee looks at the 2D image of Marie. They both notice a yellow circle over Marie's private parts.

RENEE
I gotta pat you down.

MARIE
No! It's yellow. Yellow doesn't mean
danger. It means aridity. I've had
quite the dry spell.

Marie gets the full pat down anyway.
After, she looks at Roberta who is
collecting her things.

MARIE
(to Roberta)
Well, I guess the dry spell's over.
And, now I can say I've been with a
woman.

Roberta looks at Marie with a devious
smile.

Chrisall walks up with his little shit
dog in a mesh bag. He's instructed to
put the dog on the conveyor belt.
Rodney looks at the dog on the monitor.
With its teeth lit up, the dog looks
like he's smiling. Meanwhile, Renee is
looking up the weight limit for dogs in
an x-ray machine.

RENEE
(to Rodney)
It says, "No dogs less than 10 pounds
should be placed in the x-ray machine."

They look over to the dog that has come out on the other side. Chrisall unzips the bag and gasps at his fried dog.

                    CHRISALL
                  (to Rodney)
        Aah! What did you do to Pinkie?!
                  (to Pinkie)
            Pinkie! Mon cherie!
                  (to Rodney)
        You're going to pay for this.

Chrisall starts to walk off with the bag.

                    RODNEY
                  (to Chrisall)
        You can't take that on the plane.

                    CHRISALL
              Why not?

                    RODNEY
        We don't allow Korean BBQ on the planes. The pilots don't like the smell.

Rodney tosses the bag into the confiscation bin.

                    CHRISALL
                  (to Rodney)
        I only had her a day. She was everything to me.
                  (to Pinkie)
            I'll never forget you.

Evan, a paranoid schizophrenic, walks
into the x-ray machine. The first time
it goes around him he ducks and puts
his arms over his head like something
is going to fall on his head.

                RENEE
              (to Evan)
   Sir, I'm going to need you to stay
                still.

The second time, Evan puts his hands
           over his face.

                RENEE
   Sir, I'm going to need you to stay
                still.

The third time, Evan falls into the
          fetal position.

                RENEE
Sir, do you want to make your flight or
                not?

   Evan finally complies with
         instructions.

Randall, an overweight Rambo-wannabe
walks up. Renee allows his pistol, hand
grenade, and knife. Then she talks to
          him like a mother.

                    RENEE
                 (to Randall)
Come on. What are you thinking? Cheez
Whiz? Hot dog? Can you even see your
toes? Cinnamon bun? When was the last
           time you ate a vegetable?

Renee tosses all of the food into the
garbage. Randall walks through the x-
ray machine, which beeps. Renee gives
him yet another disappointing look. It
turns out that Randall brought water
through. His water bottle is dumped and
given back to him. Randall hears
passengers in line behind him groan in
disappointment. He's holding up the
line. Randall should have known about
the water. He looks back and sees one
passenger with a tuba, one with water
ski, Burt Bacharach sits at a grand
piano, one with a 5-gallon jug of water
on one shoulder, a masked man, man
lighting cigarette with lighter, one
eating from bowl of soup, one with
badminton racquet, one with fishing
rod, one with cordless drill, one with
lit flares, one with a Viking helmet,
            and one with a drone.

Teri, Roberta, Evan, Randall, Harold,
Jimmy, Marie, and Chrisall are on their
way to the gate. Harold and his son
stop at the currency exchange booth.
Harold slides the worker a one-dollar
                    bill.

                      182

                    HAROLD
              (to currency worker)
        Hi, I'd like this exchanged for a
               hundred, please.

The currency worker gives Harold a look
of impatience. Harold laughs and high-
fives his son. Continuing to the gate,
Harold sees a woman trying to calm her
           hysterical daughter.

                AMERICAN MOTHER
                 (to daughter)
        One, two. I said, Stop! One, two,
           three. Stop! One, two, . . .

                    HAROLD
                 (to himself)
            The count doesn't work.

Then he sees a MEXICAN MOTHER trying to
               calm her son.
                 Uno, dos . . .

   Harold finds it interesting that the
    count is used in other cultures.
        And GERMAN MOTHER to her son
                Eins, zwei . . .

  And FRENCH MOTHER to her daughter
                Un, deux . . .

                    HAROLD
                 (to himself)
      The count doesn't work in any language.

CUT TO:
GATE

Teri befriends Roberta, and they sit
next to each other at the gate. They
see four Amish (?) people running
through the concourse.

TERI
They're so light-footed and fit.

ROBERTA
Yeah. And fast. Who knew?

TERI
They must be "running" late for their
flight back to Pennsylvania.

ROBERTA
Good one.

Four Arabs run by.

TERI
Oh. Either the Arabs now hate the Amish
or the first group wasn't Amish.

ROBERTA
Right. They were Hasidic Jews.

TERI
And they weren't late for a flight. I'm
Teri, by the way.

                    ROBERTA
          Roberta. Nice to meet you.

Chrisall befriends Marie and they sit
     together. They look across the
   concourse to another gate and notice
   that the flight is arriving from Las
Vegas. Next to the gate in the hallway
    is a stand where a lawyer waits for
clients. There is a sign above him that
   states "TERMINAL." There is also his
    law office sign: DISILLUSIONED LAW
SERVICES. After the passengers exit the
   plane, they line up at the law office
     stand for their wedding annulment.

                    CHRISALL
                  (to Marie)
    Look at that. Isn't that convenient.
     Poor bastards. I'm never getting
                    married.

                    MARIE
   Ditto that. And if I did, I wouldn't
   get married in Las Vegas. I would get
    married on a cliff overlooking the
       ocean, being one with nature.

                    CHRISALL
The only thing I want to be one with is
             Channing Tatum.

                    MARIE
               Count me out.

                      185

Chrisall gives her a look like he
guessed right. She's a lesbian.

                    MARIE
        Oh, yeah. Just because I do yoga and
        eat healthy I'm a lesbian. You men are
        all alike. Gay or straight. And, by the
                    way, I eat meat.

                    CHRISALL
                    So do I.

                    MARIE
            OK. When are we boarding?

                    CHRISALL
        Sorry. I'm Chrisall (offers hand shake
                as peace offering).

                    MARIE
            I'm Marie. Nice to meet you.

                    CHRISALL
        You, too. (points to a woman doing yoga
        on mat at the gate in between two rows
            of seats facing each other, near a
                        window)
                One of your friends?

        Yoga Woman is in a lunge with her back
            leg straight and she is turned
                    sideways.

                    MARIE
                That's a good one.

                      186

Chrisall and Marie continue to watch
her and their reactions change. Their
heads tilt to the left and then to the
right, like they're trying to figure
out how Yoga Woman contortioned. Then
they suddenly look aghast.

                MARIE AND CHRISALL
                      Whoa.

Yoga Woman is bent over showing her
butt to everyone in the gate when she
could have had her butt toward the
                    window.

                      MARIE
            That's contraindicated.

                    CHRISALL
        What is contra-ban or whatever you
                      said?

                      MARIE
        Contraindicated. Known to be risky.

                    CHRISALL
              More like risqué.

Randall befriends Evan and they sit
            together at the gate.

                      EVAN
                  (to Randall)
        The plane might crash, you know. I
        heard something bad is going to happen.

                    RANDALL
          Oh, yeah? Where'd you hear that?

Evan apprehensively points to his head.
Randall gives an understanding, yet
                leery nod.

                    RANDALL
     Well, not if I can help it. I'm Ramb—
     Randall. (offers hand shake) How ya'
                  doing?

                     EVAN
            (won't shake hand)
               Nervous.

Randall and Evan watch a man walk off
their plane and into the gate. The man
is already on a phone call and is very
loud and jovial. He seems like he had a
few drinks on the flight and feels no
pain. He is so distracted by his
entertaining conversation that he walks
into the women's restroom. And he
doesn't come out for five minutes. A
woman in the restroom calls 911. The
man, still on the phone, still
clueless, leaves the restroom and is
met by airport security who asks for
his ID and then escorts him out of the
                  airport.

Yoga Woman is now spread eagle on the
floor on her back with her eyes closed.
Worried Woman who didn't see Yoga Woman
exercising walks up to Yoga Woman.

                    WORRIED WOMAN
        (to Yoga Woman, standing over Yoga
                        Woman)
                    Are you OK?

                     YOGA WOMAN
        This is the true meaning of being
                      grounded.

    Worried woman thinks what she sees is
    too weird to be near and walks away to
              sit somewhere else.

    A woman with a therapy dog, Australian
    Shepherd, stops near the gate. Several
    people take turns going up to the dog.
    Of course the dog can smell everything.
        The audience hears what the dog is
                     thinking.

                    DOG
              (Australian accent)
To passenger #1: *Mmm. You smell like
               cinnamon bun.*
To passenger #2: *Gross, dude. You
didn't wash your hands after using the
          toilet. Don't pet me!*
             (to his handler)
*Remember to give me a bath when we get
                  home.*
To passenger #3: *You should wear gloves
when you fill your gas tank. Hmm.
        Diesel. Truck driver?*
To passenger #4: *Lay off the pot, dude.
You don't have cancer or seizures.*
To passenger #5: *Oh, young one. Vaping
            is smoking.*
To passenger #6: *It's a boy!*
         (pregnant/transgender joke)

   Since flight leaves at 12 p.m.,
   boarding starts at 11:30 a.m.
San Jose gate agent Kathleen gives
instructions via public address system,
but inaudible because the passengers
are not listening; they're chatting.
She realizes the public address system
isn't helpful, so she puts it down and
tries a microphone. Same effect. Then,
she takes out a bull horn. Everyone
                listens.

                    KATHLEEN
                 (on bull horn)
Good afternoon, Ladies and Gentlemen.
Uniting Air Flight 1313 to Honolulu is
   ready for pre-boarding passengers.
Anyone who needs assistance, is active
military, or is just plain pompous may
                   board now.

There is a stand four feet away from
the gate agent counter with an arrow
 pointing to the left for pre-board
passengers and groups 1-5. An arrow
points to the right for groups 6-9.

                    RANDALL
                   (to Evan)
   I used to be active military.

                     EVAN
                 You retired?

                    RANDALL
  No. Let's just say I was let go.

         Evan goes wide-eyed.

                   KATHLEEN
                 (on bull horn)
Groups 1 through 5 are welcome to board
                     now.

                     TERI
                 (to Roberta)
          What group are you?

ROBERTA
Group 7.

TERI
Me, too.

KATHLEEN
(on bull horn)
Groups 6 through 8. Welcome aboard.

The eight main passengers line up at
the end of Groups 6 through 8 in the
following order: Evan, Randall, Harold,
Jimmy, Chrisall, Marie, Teri, Roberta.
They all have to reach far to give the
gate agent their ticket, so they don't
cross the imaginary line. Gate agent
uses a trash grabber to collect the
tickets. Drone Pilot flies his plane
over the scanner, which beeps.

KATHLEEN
(to Evan)
Sir, you're going to have to check your
bag. It's too big.

EVAN
No it's not. Look.

Evan puts his bag in the carry-on
baggage sizer.

EVAN
See?

The bag is an inch too big.

KATHLEEN
Sir, your bag is too big. You're going
to have to check it.

EVAN
It fits in the overhead compartment. I
brought it on the last several flights.

KATHLEEN
I can't speak to those flights, only
this one, and I'm consistent.

EVAN
Consistently inconvenient. Why not be
consistently accommodating?

Kathleen takes his bag, places a tag on
it and gives Evan the claim check. She
resumes the boarding process.

EVAN
(to Randall)
She's going to put a bomb in my bag.

KATHLEEN
(to other passengers)
Thank you. Thank you. Welcome aboard.
Thank you. Thank you. Welcome
aboard . . .

Harold and Jimmy have been sneaking
their way back and forth over the
imaginary line. Chrisall sends his
ticket over as a paper airplane, which
is flown back to him.

KATHLEEN
(on bull horn)
Group 9 welcome aboard.

The only people in group 9 are: Captain
Tully, First Officer Wright, Navigator
Larson, Hugh, Ann, and Asian man. In
that order.

LARSON
(to Tully)
Tully, why are we always the last to
board?

TULLY
LIFO

LARSON
LIFO?

TULLY
Yeah. Remember from flight school?
LIFO. Last In First Out. Comes in handy
in the event of a water landing. This
isn't a ship we're in charge of, guys.
This is a plane. Every man for himself.
Have you ever heard of "the captain
goes down with the plane?" (They shake
their heads.) No, of course not.
Remember that.

Wright and Larson nod.

The passengers line up in the jetway.
In front of the eight main passengers
is a young teenage boy who, at the end
of the jetway, makes the sign of the
cross right before stepping into the
plane. Every other main passenger leans
to the right to see him, and the other
four lean to the left. Evan tries to
turn and run.

EVAN
(to Randall)
What does he know that we don't know?
There must be a terrorist on board.
See! Something bad is going to happen.

RANDALL
(with his hands on his sidearms)
Not if I can help it.

Harold has Jimmy on his shoulders and
takes him off and uses him as chest
protection. Chrisall crosses his
fingers, and Marie makes the meditation
sign with her fingers and mouths Om.
Teri checks herself in a compact,
because she wants to make sure she
looks good when she dies.

Roberta
(to Teri)
The sign of the cross before my exam
didn't help me. I was still diagnosed
with cancer.

ASIAN MAN
(to Hugh and Ann)
Oh, great.

Tully, Wright, and Larson try to turn
and leave the jetway, but Hugh and Ann
stop them.

HUGH
(to Tully, Wright, and Larson)
Not so fast, guys. You're taking us to
Honolulu.

TULLY
Hugh Saine, Ann Byn-Ladden?

HUGH
Yeah. Have we met? I thought you looked
familiar.

TULLY
Uh, no. No.

As Teri steps from the jetway to the
plane, she looks down through the crack
and sees two men on the tarmac holding
a safety net.

CUT TO:

CABIN

All of the passengers are in the plane and either seated or putting luggage in overhead compartments. A man is trying to fit a large suitcase up above and is shutting the lid on his bag over and over and over.

STEWARD JAN
(to non-physics professor)
You've never taken a physics class, have you? I'm going to have to check the bag for you.

Jan pulls the suitcase down and has a tug-of-war with non-physics professor over it. Jan punches him in the face, and he lets go. Jan hands him a claim check.
Harold (middle seat) and Jimmy (aisle seat, right side of plane, second to last row) are seated. They see Morbidly Obese Woman, whom they saw on the scale, walking down the aisle. Harold is thinking: *Not this row, not this row, not this row.*
Jaws theme song is heard: duh nuh duh nuh . . .

MORBIDLY OBESE WOMAN
(to Harold)
That's my seat. I have the window. (re-
checks her boarding pass) Yeah, I have
the window. You don't have to get up.
I'm sure I can just scoot by.

HAROLD
We'll get up.

Harold and Jimmy stand in the aisle,
and then they all sit.

MORBIDLY OBESE WOMAN
Sorry I'm a little large (she puts some
of her fat on top of the arm rest). I'm
afraid of flying. Sorry I'm so fat.
It's embarrassing. I need a seatbelt
extension. I eat a lot when I can't
smoke.

HAROLD
You must fly a lot.

Harold nonchalantly gives his son a
high five.

Teri (aisle seat) and Roberta are in
the last row on the right side of the
plane sitting next to a Gang Banger
(window seat) all tatted up, fresh out
of prison, and afraid of flying.

GANG BANGER
(to Teri and Roberta)
This is my first time flying.

Teri and Roberta are unsympathetic.

ROBERTA
You don't have to worry about the
pilots dying. There's a spare pilot
right there. (She points across the
aisle to Spare Pilot all suited up.)

TERI
If the plane goes down, I'll be putting
my head between *his* knees.

Evan and Randall (aisle seat) are
sitting in the last row on the left
side of the plane next to Spare Pilot.
(window seat)

RANDALL
(to Evan)
If we were any farther back we'd be on
the toilet.

EVAN
The back of the plane is the best place
to sit. It's the best place to sit.
When the wings break off, we'll still
be fine. And in a water landing, the
back of the plane is the last part to
sink. It's the last part to sink.

STEWARDESS REBECCA
(on PA)
(Passengers are quiet.) Good afternoon,
Ladies and Gentlemen. Welcome aboard
Flight 1313 to Honolulu. Please listen
carefully to these important safety
instructions. There are six emergency
exits: two at the front of the plane,
two over the wings, and two at the back
of the plane. (Passengers are loud and
talk over Rebecca.) Fasten your
seatbelt and pull on the strap, so that
the belt sits low and snug on your
waist. In the event of a water landing,
remove the life vest from underneath
your seat and place it around your
neck. Do not inflate it until you have
exited the plane. (Jan demonstrates the
instructions backwards—the seat belt
while Rebecca talks about the exits,
and the oxygen mask while Rebecca talks
about the seat belt.) Quiet! (Everyone
quiets. Jan startles.) Thank you. In
the event of loss of cabin pressure, an
oxygen mask will fall automatically
from the panel above your head.

Chrisall (middle seat) and Marie (aisle
seat) sit on the left side of the
plane, second to last row.

                    CHRISALL
                    (to Marie)
    If the plane loses cabin pressure, I
      don't want an oxygen mask to fall
    toward my head. What good is oxygen if
    the plane is about to crash? I want a
    male supermodel to land right in my lap
      (pats lap). Right here. I want to die
            with a smile on my face.

                    REBECCA
                    (on PA)
    Please turn off all portable electronic
                    devices.

                    CHRISALL
            Does a vibrator count?

                    MARIE
      Isn't it a given that all of the
      electronic devices are portable. I
    don't see anyone with a 500-mile-long
              extension cord.

                    CHRISALL
    Wouldn't it suck if you had to turn off
              your pacemaker?

                    MARIE
    Yeah. Especially if you have a fear of
                    flying.

                    TULLY
                   (on PA)
      Ladies and Gentlemen, thank you for
       flying with us. We're looking at a
      smooth flight all the way to Honolulu.
      Right now Honolulu has clear skies and
       a temperature of . . . 72 degrees.

                ALL PASSENGERS
       (disappointed, 72 degrees isn't warm
                    enough)
                      Aw.

                    TULLY
                   (on PA)
       Flight attendants prepare for takeoff.

                    EVAN
                 (to Randall)
            I'm afraid of turbulence.

                   RANDALL
      Of course you are. Turbulence is no big
        deal. It's like driving on a bumpy
      road. Ask the pilot. If he isn't afraid
       of turbulence, then you don't need to
                      be.

                    EVAN
               (to Spare Pilot)
       Excuse me. You're a pilot, right?

                 SPARE PILOT
                   Yes, Sir.

                    EVAN
        You're not a terrorist?

                 SPARE PILOT
                  No, Sir.

                    EVAN
    How much turbulence does there need to
         be for you to be scared?

    Spare Pilot gives Evan a weird look,
    because he can't imagine being scared
    by turbulence, but he thinks about it.

                 SPARE PILOT
    I guess I would be scared if the plane
    went like this (holds one hand out palm
        down and then flips hand over).

    Evan is wide-eyed and just nods and
    looks away. He is not comforted.

                   HAROLD
         (to Morbidly Obese Woman)
    (speaks like old man) Back in my day,
    the windows were crank. And that was
    first class. In coach they had casement
                  windows.

    Morbidly Obese Woman nods. She's too
    scared to hear anything else Harold
                  says.

The plane is at cruising altitude.
First class steward Brock and first
class stewardess are working in the
front of the plane. Jan and Rebecca are
preparing the snack carts at the back
of the plane. Rebecca is using an
upside-down wine bottle as an ice pick.

                    REBECCA
                   (to Jan)
Jan, the captain still calls me
stewardess. I said, "The proper term is
flight attendant." He said, "Face it.
You're just a glorified waitress." What
a jerk. He's not that great. I could do
his job. But he couldn't do ours.

                     JAN
That's right. You should tell him,
Rebecca. Tell him. Next time you talk
                   to him.

                    REBECCA
Oh, I'm going to tell him, alright.

The phone sounds and Rebecca is asked
           to go to the cockpit.

                  CUT TO:
                  COCKPIT
Rebecca brings Tully a drink.

                    REBECCA
                  (to Tully)
Here you go, Captain. Anything else?

                    TULLY
      No, that'll be all, stewardess.

                   REBECCA
      Captain Tully, I've been meaning to
                 tell you . . .

                    TULLY
                    Yes?

                   REBECCA
           Keep up the good work.

                    TULLY
      Well. Thank you. You, too. I know what
      you do is hard work. (He gives Wright
         and Larson a yeah-right look.)

         Rebecca walks out mad.

                  CUT TO:
               BACK OF PLANE

                     JAN
                (to Rebecca)
      So, did you give him a piece of your
                    mind?

                   REBECCA
      No. Maybe it's better if I don't tell
       him while the plane is still in the
                     air.

Jan nods and picks up phone to talk to
Brock. The passengers can hear the
conversation.

JAN
(to Brock)
Flight Attendant Brock, could you
please bring back a bag of cups?

BROCK
I did, already.

JAN
I still need one more.

BROCK
You didn't order enough from food
service support.

JAN
Yes, I did.

BROCK
If you didn't waste so many from the
last flight, you wouldn't need more.

Passengers are vacillating. Whose side
should they be on?

JAN
If you didn't give the first class
passengers a new cup for every sip,
then we wouldn't run out so fast.

BROCK
They pay a lot for their tickets.

First class passengers nod.
Now Brock and Jan are no longer on PA,
so they think.

JAN
(to Rebecca)
(unknowingly still on public address
system)
He's so hotty totty. He thinks that
since he gets to work first class that
he's above us. Huh. Uniting Air tells
us that the first class jobs are based
on seniority. They mean senility. I
could work first class. All you have to
do is serve more expensive food and be
a little nicer. (He realizes the public
address system is still on) Oh, never
mind. I like it back here.

An hour later, Jan and Rebecca are
about to start the snack service. A big
argument starts in the fourth-to-the-
last row on the right side of the
plane. Fit Woman is sitting in the
window seat leaning toward the window
trying to sleep. Overweight Cuban
Husband (mid-70s, middle seat) has been
digging his right elbow into the left
side of her rib cage.

FIT WOMAN
(to Cuban Husband)
Could you please move your elbow? It's
in my rib cage.

CUBAN HUSBAND
If you don't like it, you should move
over in your seat.

FIT WOMAN
(astonished) I should be able to use my
whole seat. I paid for it.

CUBAN HUSBAND
I should be able to use the arm rest.

FIT WOMAN
That's fine, but your elbow is in my
space and digging into me.

CUBAN HUSBAND
Then move over.

FIT WOMAN
If you weren't overweight, you wouldn't
be in my space.

CUBAN HUSBAND
I'm not overweight.

Cuban Wife (mid-70s, aisle seat) has
been trying for years to get her
husband to eat healthy and exercise.
She laughs hard and loud and long. She
also likes that someone finally stood
up to him, as she is not able to. Cuban
Husband and Fit Woman have a stare-
down.

CUBAN HUSBAND
You are a piece of work, Lady.

                    FIT WOMAN
                    Yes, I am.

                  CUBAN HUSBAND
              You're really something.

                    FIT WOMAN
                    Yes, I am.

       Fit Woman rings stewardess call button.
                  Jan walks over.

                    FIT WOMAN
                    (to Jan)
       He has been digging his elbow into my
       side. I asked him to move it, but he
                     won't.

                      JAN
       Well, I can't move you. This is a full
                    flight.

                    FIT WOMAN
       I'm not asking you to move me. He can
       either move his elbow, put the arm rest
        up, or change seats with his wife.

                      JAN
        The arm rest is shared space.

                    FIT WOMAN
         I don't need the arm rest!

JAN
We're all adults here. If this
bickering doesn't stop, I'm going to
have to fill out an incident report.

FIT WOMAN
Go ahead. And thanks for nothing. I
thought you were trained in conflict
resolution.

Hugh, Asian Man, and Ann are sitting in
third-to-last row, right side. They are
in the aisle, middle, and window seats,
respectively. Hugh, knowing the
conflict, stands in the aisle, punches
Cuban Husband in the face and handcuffs
Cuban Husband's right wrist to his left
arm rest, thereby pulling the elbow
away from Fit Woman.

HUGH
(to Jan)
Now that's how you resolve a conflict.

FIT WOMAN
Thank you.

HUGH
You're welcome. Just doin' my job.

Jan and Rebecca start the snack service
at the front of the main cabin and make
it as far as just forward of the middle
toilets.
Chrisall and Randall head for the
toilets at the middle of the plane.

Chrisall sees a man walk into the
bathroom with a can of club soda.
Chrisall gives Jan a curious look.

                    JAN
               (to Chrisall)
        He spilled food on his tie.

                  CHRISALL
     Oh, I thought he was going to mix
            drinks in the bathroom.
    Chrisall winks at Jan who winks back.
    Chrisall acts shy. The man walks out of
      the bathroom and Chrisall goes in.
    Randall reads the sign on the bathroom
    that Chrisall goes into: Toss Up. Then
    he reads the sign on the other bathroom
              door: Ipsigender.

                  RANDALL
                 (to Jan)
           What is ipsigender?

                    JAN
     It means that you are the same gender
          now as when you were born.

                  RANDALL
     I'm all man. Always have been, always
                 will be.

                    JAN
            I can see that.

Rebecca and Jan continue the snack service and are near the back of the plane. They hand out peanuts, drinks, and a napkin.

                    MORBIDLY OBESE WOMAN
                        (to Harold)
              Are you going to get a meal?

                         HAROLD
        No! I wouldn't eat airline food if it
              were the last meal on Earth.

                    MORBIDLY OBESE WOMAN
            You know what my last meal would be?

                         HAROLD
                    The Last Supper?

                         REBECCA
        (to Morbidly Obese Woman, Harold, and
                         Jimmy)
            What would you all like to drink?

                    MORBIDLY OBESE WOMAN
                       Diet coke.

              Harold rolls his eyes.

                         HAROLD
                 (to Rebecca and Jan)
        I'll have water, and Jimmy will have
                         milk.

                    MORBIDLY OBESE WOMAN
        What do you have in the way of meals?

REBECCA
Peanuts.

JAN
Peanuts.

REBECCA
And peanuts.

Hugh and Ann open their bags of peanuts. Asian Man didn't take a bag. Hugh and Ann start eating the peanuts. Asian Man goes into anaphylaxis.

JAN
(yells)
Does anyone have an Epi-pen?!
All of the passengers look toward Jan and hold up an Epi-pen and press the stewardess call button. DING. Hugh and Ann pull out their own Epi-pens and stab Asian Man in the thighs; he recovers.

Jan and Rebecca finish the snack service.

Creepy Guy walks out of rear bathroom and heads back to his seat. He stops at Jimmy.

CREEPY GUY
(to Jimmy)
Hey, li'l fella. What's your name?

213

JIMMY
Jimmy.

CREEPY GUY
Say, Jimmy, would you like to see my
playground?

JIMMY
Hashtag creepy. (makes # sign with
right second and third fingers over
left second and third fingers. Then, he
high-fives Harold.)

HAROLD
(to Creepy Guy)
Beat it. (to himself) Poor choice of
words.

HAROLD
(to Jimmy)
Are you ready to play with your memory
cards?

JIMMY
Yeah! Yeah!

Harold shuffles the deck and lays out
12 cards.

HAROLD
(to Jimmy)
See if you can find a match.

Jimmy lifts up cards and puts them
down.

                    HAROLD
          Remember where that is.

                    JIMMY
            I know. Look!

      Jimmy points to the window. With
      Harold's head turned Jimmy sneaks a
            peek at the cards.

                    HAROLD
                    Jimmy.

                    JIMMY
                    What?

      Jimmy resumes playing fairly and finds
                    three pairs.

                    JIMMY
            (points to window)
            Daddy, look!

                    HAROLD
          I'm not falling for that again.

                    JIMMY
            Look! Look!

            Harold looks.
                CUT TO:
              RIGHT WING
      A wing walker is doing tricks. The wing
        looks like that of a biplane.

CUT TO:
CABIN
Morbidly Obese Woman does a double take
at the wing walker and becomes
nauseated at the thought of being on
the wing.

HAROLD
Cool!

JIMMY
What is she doing, Daddy?

HAROLD
She's wing walking, son. That's how
people used to travel before planes had
more than two seats.

People nearby on the other side of the
aisle wonder what all the commotion is
and then think to look at the wing on
their side.

CUT TO:
LEFT WING
Female parachutist lands on the left
wing and tilts plane.

CUT TO:
CABIN
Everyone leans to the left and says
Whoa!

CUT TO:

LEFT WING

Parachutist takes out her breast implants, tosses them, and the plane normalizes.

CUT TO:

CABIN

Everyone looks relieved and settled, again.

A teenage girl walks to the back restrooms and passes Teri and Roberta.

TERI
(to Roberta, referring to the teenager)
The '80s called; they want their pants back.

TEENAGER
(to Teri)
The '90s called; they want your youth back.

Teri has no comeback, even though she's not that old.

TERI
(to Roberta)
So, can I ask what kind of cancer you had?

ROBERTA
Yeah. Basal cell carcinoma.

                    TERI
    Wow. That sounds terrible. I'm sorry.
            Are you terminal?

                   ROBERTA
    No. It was caught early, so I'm going
             to be fine.

                    TERI
    Well, at least it was caught early.
    Isn't that the one you get from
               smoking?

                   ROBERTA
    No, you're thinking of . . . every
            other cancer.

                    TERI
    Did you have to have surgery?

                   ROBERTA
         Yeah. Yesterday.

                    TERI
    And the doctor let you fly? Did he get
             it all?

                   ROBERTA
    Yes, the surgery was a success.

                    TERI
    Good. You must be relieved.

ROBERTA
You have no idea. This has been
weighing heavy on me. Do you want to
see the wound?

TERI
Maybe we should wait until we land. I
don't want you to undress.

ROBERTA
It's OK.

Rebecca removes her scarf and points to
the wound that's so small the camera
has to do a close-up.

TERI
(Vain) Oh, my gosh that's horrible! You
poor thing. That's much worse than I
thought it was going to be. (Checks
herself in compact) I would kill myself
if a doctor cut open my forehead.
(Hints toward plastic surgery) Well, I
guess he has already. Let me know when
it heals, and I'll send you some
concealer samples.

ROBERTA
Sure will.

TERI
So, what will you be doing in Hawaii?

ROBERTA

Visiting a friend. I booked the trip
when I was diagnosed with cancer. It
was one of those wake-up calls, you
know? Better start on my bucket list.
What's on your bucket list?

TERI

I have a kick-the-bucket list: what I'm
going to do when my uncle dies, and I
receive the inheritance. I've always
wanted to see the Alps.

ROBERTA
Oh, me, too.

TERI

I've heard that they're so beautiful,
so many vibrant colors, versatile.

ROBERTA

I know. And so picturesque. You can't
take a bad picture of the Alps.

TERI

All of my friends have seen the Alps,
but I haven't, yet. It's like a sub-
urban legend.

ROBERTA

I know. I've heard it's so striking
when you see. It's like I'll believe it
when I see it.

                    TERI
Well, of course I have seen pictures,
but I want first-hand knowledge. I just
hope it looks good on me. I'm sure it
                    will.

                  ROBERTA
You hope what looks good on you?

                    TERI
Alps. I've never tried that brand of
              makeup before.

                  ROBERTA
Makeup? I thought that you were talking
        about the mountain range.

                    TERI
There's a mountain range named after
makeup? Hmm. I guess that makes sense.

                   MARIE
              (to Chrisall)
Last night I dreamt that I dove into
the most beautiful blue pool and then I
was floating on a raft, and a bartender
    swam up and offered me a drink.

                  CHRISALL
That sounds pretty cool, actually.

                   MARIE
I have premonitions. I know the dream's
              a premonition.

                   CHRISALL
         Well, we are headed for Hawaii.

                    MARIE
     I know. That's an easy one. Anyway, I'm
     looking forward to a vacation. I need
     to re-ground myself. I just broke up
       with my boyfriend of five years.

                   CHRISALL
           Oh. Was it a bad break up?

                    MARIE
     No. It was amicable. I just wish that
     men came with a rewards card, so that
       after we break up I can get a
         percentage of my life back.

                   CHRISALL
             Where do I sign up?

                    MARIE
     I need to find a place to live when I
                   get back.

                   CHRISALL
         Are you going to buy a house?

                    MARIE
       No. I'm going to rent a house for a
     little while and then maybe buy one.

                   CHRISALL
       Well, I hope you find something.

                    MARIE
    Thanks. I'm sensing that there's an
    older woman who doesn't need to live in
              her house anymore.

                  CHRISALL
         Aw. What happens to her?

    Marie is surprised by his misplaced
      sympathy and capitalizes on it.

                    MARIE
                (to Chrisall)
       I'm going to have her evicted.

                  CHRISALL
                   What?!

                    MARIE
    Yay! You have terminal cancer. Now get
                    out!

                  CHRISALL
              Surely you jest.

                    MARIE
    Ha. No. Maybe she will move out of
      town, closer to her grandkids.

                  CHRISALL
    How do you know all this? Did you dream
                    it?

                    MARIE
    No. I just sense it. I'm an intuitive.

                     223

CHRISALL
Well, can you intuit if we will arrive
on time? (looks at watch)

EVAN
(to Randall)
What was it like?

RANDALL
What was what like? Being in the
military?

EVAN
Yeah. Were you afraid of being killed?

RANDALL
No. You learn to block it out of your
mind, so you do what you came to do.

EVAN
I could never be in the military. I
don't like to get up early.

RANDALL
Then join the Air Force.

EVAN
And I don't like to be watched.

RANDALL
We Marines are the toughest. Oorah!
Semper Fi.

EVAN
What does that mean?

RANDALL
Always loyal.

EVAN
When I was 18 I tried to join the Army,
but I didn't pass the psychological
tests.

RANDALL
I almost didn't either. I can never
remember the difference between
conscious, conscientious, and
conscience.

EVAN
Tell me more about being in the
Marines.

RANDALL
One night we were crawling on our
bellies for what seemed like an
eternity. We heard shouting and
gunfire. I was hot and thirsty, but I
couldn't take a drink. You keep your
head down. Always keep your head down.
Sweat was dripping into my eyes, and my
eyes were stinging. I could barely see.
I didn't know where I was at any given
time. I just kept following the person
in front me.

EVAN
Was there anyone behind you?

RANDALL
Yes.

EVAN
Someone was following you?

RANDALL
Yes, our platoon stayed together. We
always had each other's back.

EVAN
Then what happened?

RANDALL
We came to a creek and we had to cross
it holding our rifles out of the water—
just out of the water with our heads
low. The cool water felt good until my
muscles cramped. I almost didn't make
it out. Then we had to climb a rope 30
feet high.

EVAN
What did the rope lead to?

RANDALL
Nowhere.

EVAN
Then why did you climb it?

RANDALL
In the military you don't question
authority. You just do what you're
told.

EVAN
I didn't think they had twine in the
Middle East, just oil.

                    RANDALL
               The Middle East?

                     EVAN
        Yeah. Didn't you fight in the Persian
                    Gulf?

                    RANDALL
             No. I never saw combat.

                     EVAN
         Then where were you when you were
           crawling and crossing creeks?

                    RANDALL
                  Boot camp.

                     EVAN
                     Oh.

                    RANDALL
        Don't get me wrong. Boot camp isn't for
                the faint of heart.

                     EVAN
                 Uh huh. Hmm.

                    RANDALL
        What about you? I bet you have some
             "war" stories of your own.

        Evan gives Randall a look of wonder:
        what does Randall already know about
                     him?

HAROLD
(to Morbidly Obese Woman)
So, did you have a good weekend?

MORBIDLY OBESE WOMAN
It was OK. I went to an open house and
funeral.

HAROLD
Oh? It sounds like a busy weekend.

MORBIDLY OBESE WOMAN
Not really. The open house and funeral
were at the same time. My friend's
husband died. She is such a busy real
estate agent that she held the open
house and open casket at the same time.
She couldn't get a sitter.

HAROLD
I've never heard of that before.

MORBIDLY OBESE WOMAN
My friend's efficient. Instead of a
guest book people were signing offer
sheets.

Morbidly Obese Woman gets teary-eyed.

HAROLD
Are you OK?

MORBIDLY OBESE WOMAN
Yes. It's just that . . . my offer
wasn't accepted.

                    HAROLD
Well, you wouldn't want to buy a house
                    where—

              MORBIDLY OBESE WOMAN
        He didn't die in that house.

                    HAROLD
    Look on the bright side. You didn't
        have to go to church.

              MORBIDLY OBESE WOMAN
        (nods and wipes her nose)
            Are you married?

                    HAROLD
Jimmy's mother and I have been together
            for five years.

              MORBIDLY OBESE WOMAN
        Is she a real estate agent?

                    HAROLD
No, thank goodness. She's a dietitian.

              MORBIDLY OBESE WOMAN
                I need her.

                    HAROLD
I know. (Morbidly Obese Woman frowns.)
                Well, you—

              MORBIDLY OBESE WOMAN
I know. What's it like being married to
            a dietitian?

HAROLD
It's great. She keeps us healthy. We
eat lots of fruits and vegetables.

MORBIDLY OBESE WOMAN
Do you think she could help me?

HAROLD
Why, sure. She can help anyone even—

MORBIDLY OBESE WOMAN
What kind of diet do you think she'd
put me on?

HAROLD
That's easy. The same as anyone else:
gluten free and lactose free.

MORBIDLY OBESE WOMAN
That doesn't sound so hard.

HAROLD
And fat free, low carb., low protein.

JIMMY
Ketone free!

HAROLD
Ketone free. Grain free.

MORBIDLY OBESE WOMAN
I could do that.

HAROLD
Alcohol free. Caffeine free.

MORBIDLY OBESE WOMAN
Sure.

JIMMY
And no cat meat!

MORBIDLY OBESE WOMAN
Cat meat? Cat meat?! Who do you think I
am? Forget it! I could never give up
cat meat. I guess I'll always be fat.
Besides, Oprah said it's OK.

CHRISALL
(to Marie)
Did you hear about my dog?

MARIE
No. What happened?

CHRISALL
I had her with me. I wanted her to see
Hawaii.

MARIE
You were going to bring a dog on a
plane? Was it a service dog?

CHRISALL
No.

MARIE
Was it a therapy dog?

CHRISALL
No. Well, sort of. I get a little
anxious sometimes.

MARIE
Every dog is a therapy dog if it's
treated well. Dogs provide
unconditional love and can make people
feel calm.

CHRISALL
I know well anyways. I had to put
Pinkie, Pinkie was her name, on the
conveyor belt at the security check
point, and she went into the x-ray
machine, and, and she came out fried!
Pinkie died!

MARIE
That's awful. That happened to me once.

CHRISALL
Really?

MARIE
Yeah. I had a package of tofu dogs with
me, and they came out cooked.

CHRISALL
Pinkie was a rescue! I found her on an
adoption website.

MARIE

That's where I found my last boyfriend.
He was in a bad home, so he was mangy,
but he cleaned up well. He had a lot of
potential for being a good life-long
companion, well, for the duration of
his life; I'd outlive him. He was well-
mannered and disease-free. He came
fixed. Phew. I've paid for that
operation enough times. Still, we had
to part ways, because he didn't play
well with others.

CHRISALL

I really miss Pinkie.

MARIE

What are you going to do?

CHRISALL

I don't know. Am I wrong to be upset?

MARIE

No. It's perfectly normal. Have you
ever been to Hawaii before?

CHRISALL

No. Have you?

MARIE

Yes, you'll like it. Hawaiians are the
most open-minded Americans. Everyone
has a rainbow on their license plate.
And their car air fresheners are shaped
like a marijuana leaf.

233

CHRISALL
I tried pot once, but I didn't like it.
I don't like smelling like ass. Have
ever you tried it?

MARIE
No, I don't do drugs . . . and I live
in Napa where I have to hear about wine
all the time. Napa should plant coca
plants and experiment with cocaine
production. Locals and tourists could
go farm to farm cocaine sampling.
Customers could pair cocaine with
different types of razor blades and
mirrors. Why not? Cocaine is safer than
alcohol.

CHRISALL
Right?

MARIE
In the meantime, I will go to Georgia
for peanut butter sampling. I'm going
to bring a sterling silver knife to
spread peanut butter on artisan
crackers. I will pair peanut butter
with chocolate, pretzels, and bread,
and brag about what flavors I sense in
the peanut butter. I will attend
competitions and marvel at hand-painted
peanut butter jar labels.

CHRISALL
I love peanut butter. I love spreading
it on—

MARIE
I don't need to know. Uh. How much
longer? Isn't there a movie on this
flight?

CHRISALL
No. That would cost extra. I guess we
should just be happy that they give us
fuel.

MARIE
Did you see the tip jar at the ticket
counter?

CHRISALL
Yes, so ridiculous. I said, "Here's a
tip: smile."

MARIE
How funny. I said, "Here's a tip: stop
doing sit-ups; they're
contraindicated."

CHRISALL
Are they really? I do like two hundred
a day. Well, not all at once. When I
have time. I'm lazy. You teach yoga,
right?

MARIE

No, I'm a personal fitness trainer. I'm getting burned out though. It's time to move on. I know I've been trying to motivate lazy people for too long when I saw a potential drive-by shooting in progress, and I yelled, "If you're going to shoot someone, at least get out of the car!" I was at a self-serve car wash at the time. I thought: *Great. I'm going to be shot while cleaning my car.* The closest thing I had to a weapon was a bottle of glass cleaner. I turned the nozzle from spray to stream— just in case.

CHRISALL

How scary. (Holds up arm and jiggles arm fat) So, what can I do about this? Should I do push-ups?

MARIE

Push-ups would work your triceps. You can fill the space with muscle.

CHRISALL

Oh, no. I don't want to bulk up. I don't want to look like a professional wrestler.

MARIE

Ha. Don't worry. No one will ever mistake you for a professional wrestler. I promise you that.

CHRISALL
So, what should I do? Are dips good?

MARIE
I can tell you what exercises are
effective and how to do them safely,
but I can't say what *you* should do,
because I don't know enough about you.

CHRISALL
By the time we get to Hawaii you will.

MARIE
Yeah.

CHRISALL
Well, can you tell me what the best
exercise is?

MARIE
That which is done.

CHRISALL
What's the best time of day to
exercise?

MARIE
When you will do it.

CHRISALL
Oh, you're one of those.

MARIE
One of what?

CHRISALL
The ethical type. There's-no-easy-way-
out type.

MARIE
Yep.

HAROLD
(to MORBIDLY OBESE WOMAN)
So, what do you do?

MORBIDLY OBESE WOMAN
I was on the Ellen Degeneres show
three, no four times.

HAROLD
Really? What were you doing?

MORBIDLY OBESE WOMAN
I gave Ellen several pieces of my art.

HAROLD
When you were on stage you were showing
your art?

MORBIDLY OBESE WOMAN
I wasn't on stage.

HAROLD
Then what were you doing?

MORBIDLY OBESE WOMAN
Nothing. I was just in the audience. I
manifested it to happen. When my phone
rang I knew it was Ellen calling to
tell me that I was going to be on the
show. I willed it to happen.

HAROLD
Ellen herself called you?

MORBIDLY OBESE WOMAN
No. One of her producers.

HAROLD
So, what were you actually doing in the
audience?

MORBIDLY OBESE WOMAN
Just watching the show, but I gave
Ellen several pieces of my art.

HAROLD
Do you know how many gifts she must
receive? I'm sure she sees less than 1%
of what she's given.

MORBIDLY OBESE WOMAN
Oh, no. I know she saw it. I visualized
her holding and looking at my art. And,
I sent some to Disney.

HAROLD
Yes, I'm sure the same thing happens at
Disney.

MORBIDLY OBESE WOMAN
Oh. I know they looked at it, because I
applied for a job. You can't submit
work unless you apply for a job.
They'll like the one I sent of Pluto.

HAROLD
Yes, they'll like it after they
consider it a copyright infringement.

MORBIDLY OBESE WOMAN
I'm not going to sell it. I just want
them to buy it and use it for
merchandising.

HAROLD
Do you know what Walter Disney started
out doing?

MORBIDLY OBESE WOMAN
He was a visionary?

HAROLD
No, he was a cartoonist.

MORBIDLY OBESE WOMAN
Oh, I know.

JIMMY
Uh, biddi biddi biddi "That's all
folks!"
(from *Looney Tunes*)

ROBERTA
(to GANG BANGER)
Would you like a slice of watermelon?

GANG BANGER

Oh, ya' think that cuz I'm Black I must like watermelon. "Offer da Black man watermelon." Ya' want me to get on a table 'n' do a hambone?

Roberta is stunned and can't get in a word edgewise, but is speechless anyway.

GANG BANGER
No. I just ate.

ROBERTA
What'd you have?

GANG BANGER
Fried chicken.

ROBERTA
Oh, did you have the beer-battered chicken?

GANG BANGER
No! I don't want no beer batter. I tol' 'em, "Dat better not be no beer-battered chicken." Dey gave me beer-battered chicken las' time.

ROBERTA
Did you get drunk?

GANG BANGER
No.

                    ROBERTA
              You don't like alcohol?

                  GANG BANGER
        I have a drink once in a while. Ya'
        know. In social setting. But, I don't
        want no alcohol in my food. Der better
        not be no beer in my fried chicken.

                    HAROLD
                (to Gang Banger)
        What if the chicken were fed beer?

                  GANG BANGER
                     No.

                    RANDALL
                (to Gang Banger)
        What if the chicken ate barley?

                  GANG BANGER
        I don't want no alcohol in my food.

                    ROBERTA
                    Got it.
                   (to Teri)
              Would you like a slice?

                     TERI
        No, thanks. I had grapefruit for
                   breakfast.

                    ROBERTA
              And nothing else?

TERI
Mm hm.

ROBERTA
Grapefruit isn't a meal. It's more like
a palate cleanser.

TERI
(flips through a fashion magazine and
points to a woman)
I bet she eats grapefruit for
breakfast.

ROBERTA
And you think she looks good? She looks
fresh out of Auschwitz.

TERI
I should go *there* next.

ROBERTA
Auschwitz is a concentration camp where
Jews were sent.

TERI
That's why they're so good at business.

ROBERTA
I, I, I am Jewish and I—

TERI
Are you good at business?

ROBERTA
Well, no, but—

                    TERI
          Have you been to Auschwitz?

                   ROBERTA
              No. Of course not.

                    TERI
Well, that's why. You need to learn to
concentrate. We'll go together. (Looks
up and down the aisle) When is the
   snack cart coming around again?

Roberta shakes her head, baffled by her
              seat mates.

                    TERI
          What do you do for work?

                   ROBERTA
I don't work. I retired right before I
got sick. I was a sociology professor.

                    TERI
       Oh. Cool. Did you like it?

                   ROBERTA
I did, but I didn't like the other
              professors.

                    TERI
               Why not?

                    ROBERTA
    They weren't very supportive of the
    students. One didn't even want to
    teach. She just wanted to conduct
research. Another was such a prude, she
got nervous every time a student asked
    a serious question. I always dreaded
walking by the student advising office.
    Every time I walked by when it was
    open, I'd see a student walk out
    crying. And then there's tenure.

                     TERI
                What's that?

                    ROBERTA
    Job security for those who chose the
wrong profession. The department was an
interesting sociological experiment in
and of itself. I'm not sure if it were
        more like the Stanford Prison
        Experiment or Milgram's obedience
experiment. A student told me that in
    one of her classes when papers were
passed back, she only received a small
    piece of scratch paper with her name
        and "0 out of 50." She had a big
argument with the professor, who said
    that she didn't turn in a paper. The
student told him he must have lost it.

                     TERI
              Oh, how awful.

ROBERTA

The professor told the student, "I've never lost a paper in my entire career." The student told him, "Well now you have. And in my entire education, I have never turned in an assignment late, let alone not at all."

TERI

So, then what happened?

ROBERTA

A week later during class, the professor interrupted himself and told the student, "I found something of yours" and laughed.

TERI

He laughed?

ROBERTA

Yes. And the professor took off five points for turning in the paper late. But the paper wasn't turned in late; it was found late.

TERI

Wow. That's really bad. I was late once.

ROBERTA
Okay.

TERI

It turned out I miscounted the weeks. Ooh. That was scary.

                    ROBERTA
        I don't have to worry about that
                    anymore.

                     TERI
              Because you're old?

                    ROBERTA
        Chemotherapy. It causes infertility.
         It's OK. I have two grown boys.

                     TERI
                  That's nice.

                   RANDALL
                  (to Evan)
        So, what about it? Do you have war
                   stories?

                     EVAN
        Well, I'm always at war with my next-
               door-neighbor.

                   RANDALL
        Ugh. Neighbors. Good ones are hard to
                  come by.

                     EVAN
        He has a vendetta against my pine trees
        that line our fence. He cut a branch a
                  year ago.

                   RANDALL
             OK. Why was that bad?

                    EVAN
He didn't like that it was hanging over
the fence into his yard. The tree could
have died. You have to cut branches a
certain way. You have to cut 'em a
             certain way.

                   RANDALL
           How big was the branch?

                    EVAN
(motions with two fingers, circle about
an inch in diameter) About this big
                  around.

                   RANDALL
               That's it?

                    EVAN
  Yeah, but you have to cut branches a
certain way. So, now every time he goes
outside, I guard the pine trees. But, I
can't always be at the fence. When I'm
sleeping he cuts more branches. I swear
  I saw pairs of branches in a (motions
with forearms) cross position, stuck in
the ground. His backyard looked like a
         pine tree branch cemetery.

                   RANDALL
Maybe they were branches from one of
               his trees.

                    EVAN
          I don't think so.

                    RANDALL
              Are they still there?

                      EVAN
    No. Last month I thought I heard him
   talking on the phone with someone about
     the trees. He was motioning like he
   wanted to cut all the trees down. So,
      the next day I trimmed all of the
                     trees.

                    RANDALL
          How'd that work out for you?

                      EVAN
    Terrible. Now he can see into my yard.
       I think he's always watching me.

                    RANDALL
    Well, aren't you always watching him?

                      EVAN
       I have to guard the pine trees. I
    installed a motion sensor, so now when
   he gets close to the fence, an alarm in
                my house sounds.

                    RANDALL
    Did you ever think to ask him how he
           feels about the trees?

                      EVAN
                      No.

                    RANDALL
Ask him. Maybe there was a problem with
just one branch, and you blew it out of
                  proportion.

                     EVAN
No. I was a prison guard. I know how to
                 read people.

                    RANDALL
           Really?! (stunned) I, I—

                     EVAN
I worked at Federal Prison, Alderson.

                    RANDALL
Alderson, Alderson. Why does that name
      sound familiar? Where is it?

                     EVAN
            It's in West Virginia.

                    RANDALL
Oh!! That's right. That's a minimum
security prison . . . (now totally
        unimpressed) for women.

                     EVAN
Women are tough to watch. Tougher than
                you think.

                    RANDALL
(still unimpressed) Uh huh. Oh, that's
where Martha Stewart served her
                  sentence.

                         EVAN
Yeah. We were there at the same time. I
met her. I mean I didn't just meet her.
I saw her every day that she was in the
    joint, because I guarded her wing.

                       RANDALL
              What was she like?

                         EVAN
She smelled like . . . snickerdoodles,
the kind with a Hershey's Kiss in the
middle. Martha . . . she let me call
    her Martha . . . overhauled the
prison's kitchen: taught everyone how
  to cook, created healthy menus, and
color-coded the pots and pans so that
    people knew what to use for each
recipe. Did you know that (looks around
    to see if anyone is listening and
  whispers) one crème brûlée (motions
size of custard dish) has a <u>tablespoon</u>
                 of sugar?!

                       RANDALL
              No. How was it?

                         EVAN
I didn't eat it. I was afraid it might
      have . . . that someone might
have . . . it smelled good. Martha even
changed Alderson from Alderson Prison
       to Alderson Prison Camp.

RANDALL
Did you meet anyone else famous while
you worked for the prison? How long did
you work there?

EVAN
A year. I quit, because the other
guards were up to something. I think
they were trying to get me fired.
Whenever I saw them talking, they'd
look over to me and laugh.

RANDALL
And you figured they were talking about
you? I used to think like that. And
then I graduated from high school.

EVAN
Where'd you go to high school?

RANDALL
In San Jose.

EVAN
Which high school?

RANDALL
St. Catharine's. It's an all gir—(Evan
goes wide-eyed. Randall is actually a
woman?) It's a Catholic school.

EVAN
I remember SC. We played them in field
hockey.

                    RANDALL
          You played field hockey?

                     EVAN
            No. I just watched.

                    RANDALL
     Oh, I was going to say. I don't
remember you. I played all four years.

                     EVAN
Wait. SC had a men's field hockey team?

                    RANDALL
   It was uh, uh, progressive school.
Look! (points out window to change the
               subject) A cloud!

                     EVAN
                   (startled)
               Don't do that.

                 SPARE PILOT
                  (to Evan)
             It's just a cloud.

                   CHRISALL
                  (to Marie)
                I'm bored.

                     MARIE
Me, too. Ha. Me, too. Hashtag me, too.
    Did the Me Too movement start out of
                  boredom?

CHRISALL
(quoting others) I'm bored. Me, too.
Let's complain about sexual harassment.

MARIE
I won't be friends with anyone who says
hashtag.

CHRISALL
Right? Don't speak in symbols or
abbreviations. And stop making your
hands into the shape of a heart.

MARIE
My entire life I have always believed
that I was at an advantage for being a
woman. Of course I wouldn't have
thought that 100 years ago, but I've
lived in the late 20th and early 21st
centuries. Why are women whining about
being at a disadvantage?

CHRISALL
Try being gay.

MARIE
I know. You would think that being
feminine would help you, but . . .
you're a man being feminine.

CHRISALL
I know. Believe me, I know. Well, it is
what it is. You know?

                    MARIE
      No, I don't know. (Chrisall looks at
         Marie confused) You didn't say
                  anything.

                   CHRISALL
           I said it is what it is.

                    MARIE
      I know. That's a bunch of nothingness.
       It's a poor use of the English
                  language.

                   CHRISALL
         OK, Mrs. Mary Ann Webster.

                    MARIE
      Merriam-Webster. (Chrisall rolls his
       eyes) I'm sorry. I just hate that
      phrase. So, when did you know you were
                    gay?

CUT TO:

FLASHBACK, CHRISALL'S CHILDHOOD

[Voiceover] Not until I was much older. I had a pretty normal childhood. I was like every other boy. I played with action figures . . . (Show him at 5 years old playing with two other boys who have G.I. Joes. Chrisall presents Barbie and neatens her dress and puts on her shoes. The two other boys scoff and one punches Chrisall.) . . . I rode bikes with my friends . . . (Show him at 10 years old on a bike with a basket and tassels hanging from the handle bars. One of two boys rides toward Chrisall and punches him and Chrisall falls off his bike.) . . . played video games . . . (Show him at 13 years old dancing to an interactive dance video. Two other boys are with him, sitting on the couch facing the TV. One gets up and punches Chrisall and then puts on a video where he and the other boy can blow things up.) . . . played music . . . (Show Chrisall at 17 years old playing a triangle. One of his two friends punches Chrisall and the two friends start playing electric guitars.)

[Through the years it's the same two friends.]

CUT TO:
CABIN

                    MARIE
I see what you mean. So, when did you
know? Have you told your parents, yet?

                  CHRISALL
They knew all along. (Re-show all four
flashback scenes; this time pan to his
 parents after each time Chrisall is
punched. His parents have their arms
 folded at their chests and they're
        shaking their heads.)

                    MARIE
      So, when did you know?

                  CHRISALL
Right before I went off to college. My
parents sat me down and had a heart-to-
              heart talk.

                 CUT TO:
        CHRISALL'S LIVING ROOM
Chrisall stands with his parents. His
dad punches him, his mother gives him a
Playgirl Magazine, and they send him on
his way. They all wave goodbye. After
Chrisall drives away, his parents take
turns slapping each other, blaming each
      other for having a gay son.

                 CUT TO:
                 CABIN

MARIE
How nice that your parents were so
open, honest, and accepting.

CHRISALL
Uh, huh. So, what are you going to do
when you get back to California if you
don't want to be a trainer anymore?

MARIE
I'm going to try the tech field. It
pays well. I'll start out applying for
contract positions. Those are usually
three months long.

CHRISALL
Three months seems manageable.

MARIE
There's no paid vacation time, but
there's plenty of unpaid time off.

CHRISALL
It's called being let go. I have
engineer friends in San Diego, who work
biotech. They work for a new company
for a couple of years, hope for the
company's product to be successful, and
then wait for the company to be bought
out. My friends get laid off, accept a
severance package, take a year off of
work, and then go onto the next job.

MARIE
Wow. That's amazing. I need to find a
job where I don't have to work.

CHRISALL
Start your own business.

MARIE
Hmm. I think you might be onto
something.

CHRISALL
I thought about making my own scarves.

MARIE
Silk scarves or winter scarves?

CHRISALL
Either. Both. Something for everyone.
(Motions like he's picturing . . .) I
want to have my own shop. Over here
would be hickey scarves, and over there
would be double chin scarves, and there
would be a table of Adam's apple
scarves for transgender women,
tracheotomy scarves.

MARIE
You should do it. What would you call
your store?

CHRISALL
(thinks about it)
Scarf You.

MARIE
I like it. (puts one hand on the front
of her neck) Can I order a turning 40
scarf?

259

                    EVERYONE
              (gasps and looks at Marie)
                   You're 40?!

Marie isn't sure if they think that's
old or if they think she looks young
              for 40.

                     MARIE
              How old are you now?

                    CHRISALL
                    I'm 23.

                     MARIE
              Oh, you're just a pup.

                    CHRISALL
              A pup with a plan.

                     MARIE
I respect that. You have a lot going
for you and plenty of time to do it.
Speaking of plan, what are you going to
              do in Hawaii?

                    CHRISALL
Meet up with friends from college.
We're going to do the usual touristy
stuff: get drunk, drop beer bottles
from our hotel room balcony, get kicked
              out of our hotel.

                     MARIE
Oh, there are so many fun things to do
on Oahu. Surf, snorkel, hike—

CHRISALL
Why would I want to exercise in Hawaii?
I'm going there to relax. I'm on
vacation! The most exercise I'll be
getting is waving the pool bartender
over to my raft.

MARIE
I'm going on a glider ride. It's so
fun. I've done it before. Well, I went
with the wrong person, though. He got
airsick. He turned green. It was funny
until he threw up all over me.

CHRISALL
Uh. Gross. You just reminded me that I
get air sick.

MARIE
The stewardesses should offer ginger
ale.

CHRISALL
That's not a bad idea, actually.

Marie looks up and down the aisle for
the stewardess. Chrisall rings the
stewardess call button. Rebecca walks
up, turns it off, and returns to the
back of the plane.

                    MORBIDLY OBESE WOMAN
                         (to Harold)
         I was once stuck on The Grapevine for
         <u>four</u> hours. I didn't have anything to
                 eat and I was out of smokes.

         Harold realizes Morbidly Obese Woman is
                      talking to him.

                    MORBIDLY OBESE WOMAN
         Oh, and I had to pee so bad. People
         started walking up and down the
         highway, and police were telling them
         to get back in their cars. But, what
         else were we supposed to do?

                         HAROLD
                       (uninterested)
                         Uh huh.

                    MORBIDLY OBESE WOMAN
         Then, I never thought I'd say this
         (looking off, picturing it like a
         rainbow), but the most beautiful sight
                 appeared. Biffies.

                         HAROLD
                        Biffies?

                    MORBIDLY OBESE WOMAN
              Yeah. Biffies. You know . . .
         outhouses, Johnnies, porta potties.

                         HAROLD
         I know what a biffy is. On the freeway?

                            262

MORBIDLY OBESE WOMAN
Yeah. A flatbed truck that happened to
be hauling biffies stopped alongside
the road. The driver let us use 'em.
What a godsend, I'll tell ya'.

HAROLD
Now that's an emergency vehicle. Being
guys, though, we don't really need help
with that. But, what would really help
me is if a playground showed up. It's
difficult enough for kids to sit in the
car when we're going somewhere, but
when we're stopped . . . I'd love to
see a flatbed truck with a jungle gym
pull up.

MORBIDLY OBESE WOMAN
Well, I don't exercise so . . . (Harold
stops listening to her).

Harold realizes his son isn't sitting
next to him. Harold looks up and down
the aisle and sees Jimmy at the front
of the plane walking toward the back,
holding a tray with a strap attached
that is going around his neck. The tray
is full of cigars and cigarettes.

JIMMY
Cigars, cigarettes, cigarillos. Cigars,
cigarettes, cigarillos. Cigars,
cigarettes, cigarillos. (Jimmy collects
cash and hands out products.) Cigars,
cigarettes, cigarillos.

MORBIDLY OBESE WOMAN
Is he OK? What is he doing?

HAROLD
He's selling. That's my boy.

MORBIDLY OBESE WOMAN
What's he selling?

HAROLD
Cigars and cigarettes.

MORBIDLY OBESE WOMAN
He's selling smokes?! Ah! I would kill
to have a cigarette. Get him back here.

Harold motions Jimmy back to his seat.
Jimmy returns without the tray.

HAROLD
How'd you do?

JIMMY
Sold out.

HAROLD
That's my boy.

Passengers are shown with cigars and
cigarettes in their mouths and they're
about to light up. Ann and Hugh put a
cigarette in Asian Man's mouth much to
his delight. Everyone is about to light
up by striking a match, but a sign
comes on: ("Ding" sound effect) Don't
even think about it.

                    MORBIDLY OBESE WOMAN
            Hey, kid, Can I get ultra slim?

                         JIMMY
                       Not likely.

        Harold and Jimmy nonchalantly high-five
                      each other.

                    MORBIDLY OBESE WOMAN
                      So close but—

                         HAROLD
        No cigar? Have you ever tried hypnosis?

                    MORBIDLY OBESE WOMAN
            Yes, but not for smoking. It was to
        help me get over my fear of dogs. I
                couldn't get near 'em.

                         HAROLD
                      Can you now?

                    MORBIDLY OBESE WOMAN
                          No.

                         HAROLD
                  So, nothing changed.

                    MORBIDLY OBESE WOMAN
            Well, one thing. It's strange. Now
        whenever I hear a bell I salivate.

                         HAROLD
        By any chance was the hypnotist's name
                     Dr. Pavlov?

                    MORBIDLY OBESE WOMAN
                           Who?

                         HAROLD
                       Dr. Pavlov?

                    MORBIDLY OBESE WOMAN
          Oh, I don't know. I couldn't understand
          anything he said. He spoke with a thick
                    Russian accent.

                         ROBERTA
                        (to Teri)
          I wasn't supposed to be on this flight.
             I guess everything happens for a
          reason. I had family issues and had to
            leave later than planned. Geez. You
               wouldn't believe what I had to go
             through to change my ticket. I had to
          give them everything except the name of
                      my first born.

                          TERI
          I don't have a first born, but I have a
            first aborted. What was the family
               issue . . . if you don't mind me
                         asking?

                        ROBERTA
          Well, I've already told you more than I
            would normally tell a stranger, but I
            guess that goes with the territory of
               flying. What happened was—

                    TERI
      Oh, I had a family issue, too. We had
      to put my grandmother in a long-term
                care facility.

                   ROBERTA
               Oh, which one?

                    TERI
                 Cedarwood.

                   ROBERTA
      Cedarwood. Cedarwood. Why does that
       sound familiar? Oh, isn't that a
                  cemetery?

                    TERI
      Yeah. So, what was the family issue?

                   ROBERTA
      My nephew got married. The wedding date
      was changed, and that's why I had to
                change my flight.

                    TERI
          How is that a family issue?

                   ROBERTA
      I guess it was less of an issue and
              more of a funeral.

                    TERI
      What? It was depressing or was everyone
                wearing black?

ROBERTA

No, I just think of marriage as a death
sentence. I guess I'm jaded because I
was married once. My husband didn't do
anything wrong. In fact, he was great.
Just not great enough. I realized I
prefer women.

TERI
(mouth drops and eyes bug out)
You wanted a woman to marry you?

ROBERTA
Something like that.

TERI
I didn't know there was such a thing as
a female priest.

ROBERTA
No. Yeah. Uh, no. What?

TERI
Ever since I was a little girl I have
dreamed about my fairy tale wedding. I
would marry Prince Charming, of course,
and wear a beautiful white gown—

ROBERTA
White?

                    TERI
. . . with a long train like Princess
Diana's. We would marry in a cathedral,
one with a male priest, of course. Our
reception would be held in a castle and
we would honeymoon in the Virgin
                   Islands.

                  ROBERTA
Ha. Virgin Islands. That's ironic.

                    TERI
                   What?

                  ROBERTA
Where would you and Prince Charming
    live, in Barbie's townhouse?

                    TERI
Hmm. I'm not sure it's big enough.

                  ROBERTA
I think of marriage as a probationary
period until divorce. I had medical
     coverage but no other perks.

                    TERI
(examining her left hand) I would get
   my wedding ring tattooed . . . in
pencil . . . just in case, well, you
  know. I'm young. I could get my big
break. What I'm most looking forward to
 is the bachelorette party. Those are
   always so fun. My favorite game is
    guess who's going home with the
   stripper. That'll be on a Monday.

                    ROBERTA
                What do you mean?

                     TERI
        I want to have a whole week's worth of
        parties. Ha ha. OK. So, on Sunday would
          be the engagement party. Monday the
          bachelorette party, Tuesday the bridal
           shower, Wednesday the wedding.

                    ROBERTA
         Wait. Why would the wedding be on a
        Wednesday? Doesn't it make more sense
               to have it on a weekend?

                     TERI
        No. Wednesday starts with wed. Anyway,
        Thursday would be the honeymoon, and
              Friday would be the—

                    ROBERTA
                 Baby shower?

                     TERI
        Opening of gifts, and Saturday would be
                     the—

                    ROBERTA
                 Annulment?

                     TERI
          No, silly. Returning the gifts.

                    ROBERTA
Well, it sounds like you have it all
figured out. I just think of marriage
as lactose. Humans weren't supposed to
    tolerate it but some people do.

                     TERI
Now I just need to find a man. I wonder
if the pilot's single. He has a secure
   job. Nothing could ever go wrong.

     There's a bump of turbulence.

                     TERI
   Speaking of lactose, where's the
stewardess? I'm thirsty. (Teri looks up
          and down the aisle.)

                    ROBERTA
  Sorry, but I'm all talked out. I'm
      going to turn on a movie.

                     TERI
 Good idea. What one are you going to
                watch?

                    ROBERTA
   Lincoln. I'll watch anything with
          Daniel Day Lewis.

                     TERI
 Oh! Isn't that the one where the girl
writes notes, you know. She has a crush
 on her boss. Who doesn't? And she's
        trying to get healthy.

                      271

ROBERTA
Bridget Jones's Diary?

TERI
Yeah! That's it!

ROBERTA
No.

TERI
I love that movie. Good idea. That's
what I'll watch.

ROBERTA
I wouldn't watch that movie if I were
stuck in an airport overnight.

TERI
You were stuck in an airport overnight?

ROBERTA
No, I—

TERI
(finds movie on her phone)
Yay! I found it!

Hugh and Ann stand part way and look
back toward Teri and Roberta.
ANN
(to Teri and Roberta)
We watched that movie last night.

HUGH
It was great!

Asian Man hits his head against the
                    seat.

                    ANN
           We love Rene Zellweger.

                    HUGH
        We've watched her <u>whole</u> catalog.

                    ANN
                   Twice.

               GANG BANGER
             (shakes his head)
               White people.

                    HUGH
     You'll love the part where—oh, I won't
                give it away.

                  ROBERTA
               It's OK. I—

                    TERI
            I've seen it before.

                  ROBERTA
        I'm going to watch *Lincoln*.

                    ANN
          Isn't that the one where—

     There's another bump of turbulence and
     the fasten seatbelt sign goes on. Hugh
     and Ann sit back down and fasten their
                  seatbelts.

                         EVAN
                    (to Randall)
        We're going down, the plane's going to
            crash, we're going down.

                     SPARE PILOT
        Think of turbulence as a speed bump
        that you drive over. You can feel it,
            but it doesn't hurt you.

                       RANDALL
        Let's see if the (pushes stewardess
        call button) stewardess can convince
            you that everything's fine.

        Rebecca, standing in the galley,
        reaches out a stick with a hand
        attached to the far end and uses it to
        turn off the call button. Randall looks
                    back annoyed.

                         EVAN
            Did you hear what I said?

                       RANDALL
        Yes, you said that your mother didn't
        let you play outside when you were a
        child and your only friend was
                    imaginary.

        Evan looks at Randall like, how did he
                 know, kind of.

                         EVAN
                  They're real.

                          274

RANDALL
(changes the subject)
So, why are you going to Hawaii?

EVAN
I needed a vacation and I heard that it
was a good place to relax. Uh. I'm
thirsty. How much longer do we have?

RANDALL
Who told you it was a good place
to . . . (Randall sees Spare Pilot
shake his head) never mind. (to Spare
Pilot) Hey, Captain. How many flight
hours you logged?

SPARE PILOT
Oh, I'm in the tens of thousands.

RANDALL
You get the long hauls.

SPARE PILOT
Yes. I was just in California visiting
family. I do the Honolulu to Tokyo
flights.

RANDALL
That's a good gig.

Hugh and Ann stand up part way and look
back toward Spare Pilot, Evan, and
Randall.

HUGH
(to Spare Pilot)
Hey. We might be on your flight. (to
Ann) We're going to Tokyo, right?

ANN
(she looks at Asian Man and then at
Hugh)
I don't know. They all look alike.

ASIAN MAN
You American all racist.

ANN
I mean. We don't have our orders, yet.

Jimmy notices Hugh's and Ann's badges.
He points his finger at Hugh's badge
and tries to read it.

JIMMY
Huh. Huh. Hugh Saine. Hugh Saine. (Then
points to Ann's badge) Ann bine. Bine.
Bin. Bin Laden. Ladden. Ann Byn-Ladden.
(points to Hugh's badge) Hugh Saine,
(points to Ann's badge) Ann Byn-Ladden.

TERI
(to Hugh and Ann)
Hugh Saine, Ann Byn-Ladden?

EVAN
Hugh Saine, Ann Byn-Ladden? Hugh Saine,
Ann Byn-Ladden are on the plane!?

Everyone starts screaming.

                    HUGH
Everyone calm down. Calm down. Quiet!
    We're CIA agents transporting a
                  criminal.

Everyone screams again.

                    ANN
    It's OK. He's Asian.

Everyone screams again.

                    ANN
         East Asian.

Everyone is fine with that.

Jan and Rebecca sit in the back of the
    plane, totally oblivious to the
commotion; they take a break and chat.

                    JAN
    I got so drunk last night.

                  REBECCA
    Cool! What happened?

                    JAN
We flew into Reno. Remember I said I
    flew from Reno to San Jose this
               morning?

                  REBECCA
         Yeah.

JAN

Yeah. That's where a few of us partied.
It was so fun. I had like seven shots
of tequila. I think I'm still a little
drunk.

REBECCA

Probably. Good thing Uniting Air
doesn't do random drug testing.

JAN

I know. I'd be random using someone
else's urine.

REBECCA

Right? I met someone.

JAN

A one-night stand isn't "meeting
someone."

REBECCA

No. We went out like twice. He's really
nice. I think he's the one.

JAN

The one with a job?

REBECCA

Yeah. I mean I really like him. And he
doesn't work for Uniting Air, so I
wouldn't have to see him like all the
time, you know?

                    JAN
I know. It sucks to have to see someone
          you really like.

                  REBECCA
You know what I mean. I mean I can like
meet other guys in case he's not the
              right one.

                    JAN
     You just said he's the one.

                  REBECCA
Well, he's better than the last one.
Remember? He said, "You're my number
two." Number two?! I don't want to be
number two! I want to be his number
four—the clean-up hitter. The one who
sends the first three home and then is
hailed for it. I don't know why you
              date men.

                    JAN
One good thing about LGBTQ is that it
gives us more than two genders to
        choose from, you know?

                  REBECCA
Yeah. I should keep my options open.
What would it be called if you and I
              dated?

                    JAN
            A disaster.

ROBERTA
(walks back to Jan and Rebecca)
Can I please get some coffee?

JAN
Yeah, we're just about to start the
beverage service . . . *again*.

Roberta walks back to her seat.

JAN
(rolls his eyes and lets out a big
sigh)
This job would be great if it weren't
for the passengers.

REBECCA
And the pilots.

They high-five each other.

The snack cart, making its second
round, is as far as Hugh, Ann, and
Asian Man.

REBECCA
(to Hugh, Ann, and Asian Man)
What would you like to drink?

HUGH
Water.

ANN
Water.

ASIAN MAN
Coffee.

Rebecca serves the water first and then
the coffee. There's turbulence, and she
spills the coffee on Asian Man.

ASIAN MAN
AAaaaaaa!!!!!

Hugh and Ann pour their water on his
lap.

ASIAN MAN
Alright. Alright. I talk. But first I
have to pee.

ANN
Uuuuggghhhh. Alright. Let's go.

Hugh, Ann, and Asian Man head for the
toilet in the back of the plane. Asian
Man walks into the bathroom.

CUT TO:
INT. REAR BATHROOM
Asian Man is relaxed, peeing.

CUT TO:
INT. HONOLULU AIR TRAFFIC CONTROL
TOWER
Radar looks normal, lucky for Air
Traffic Controller Earhardt (speaks
pidgin) who dozed off. His supervisor
walks up to him.

                    SUPERVISOR
                   (to Earhardt)
              Earhardt! How's it?

                    EARHARDT
         Fine. Fine. Everyt'ing look good.

                    SUPERVISOR
            Good. Keep it that way.

                    EARHARDT
                   Yes, sir.
         Supervisor walks away and Earhardt goes
          back to sleep. Radar: planes zig zag,
             narrowly avoiding one another.

                    CUT TO:
                    COCKPIT
                    TULLY
                    Birds!

         Three hummingbirds flutter inside the
          cockpit. Tully, Wright, and Larson put
           their bent arms up to their faces to
         avoid being hit by one. It looks like a
                 scene from *The Birds*.

                    CUT TO:
                  EXT. PLANE
         The plane flies erratically, because no
          one is holding onto the controls.

                    CUT TO:
            CABIN, REAR BATHROOM

Asian Man is peeing all over the bathroom and himself.

CUT TO:
CABIN, REAR

EVAN
(to Randall)
I knew we were going to die!

RANDALL
Let's roll.

Chinese Man with badminton racquet and Randall quickly walk up to the cockpit and enter. Chinese Man swipes at the hummingbirds like they're shuttlecocks. He misses. Randall grabs him and pushes him out of the cockpit.

RANDALL
(to Chinese Man)
Move!

Randall makes three kill shots—one per bird. He feels proud, but not for long.

WRIGHT
What are you doing?!

LARSON
What are you mental?!

TULLY
Get out!!

Each bullet went through a bird and then through the cockpit window. The plane loses pressure and descends rapidly.

RANDALL
Oops.

Randall exits cockpit and returns to his seat. The cockpit becomes very loud and there is debris everywhere like being in a tornado. It is difficult for Tully, Larson, and Wright to hear or see one another.

TULLY
(to Earhardt)
(yelling) Honolulu this is Captain Tully on Flight 1313. We just had a bird strike, and we're going to need assistance.

EARHARDT
Roger dat, Flight 1313. Bird strike. Which engine you lose?

TULLY
None. We have three bullet holes in the cockpit windows. Long story.

CUT TO:
INT. HONOLULU AIR TRAFFIC CONTROL TOWER

                    SUPERVISOR
                   (to Earhardt)
            What's going on, Earhardt?

                     EARHARDT
        Flight 1313 headed for Honolulu had
        bird strike and has t'ree bullet hole
               in cockpit window.

                    SUPERVISOR
        That's the strangest thing I've ever
        heard. Alright, see if they can make it
                    to Maui.

                     EARHARDT
         Flight 1313, you make it to Maui?
        Kahului, Kapalua both have runway
                number 1 open.

                      TULLY
        Negative. We're losing altitude fast.

                     EARHARDT
        Kona, Hilo? I clear runway 2 for you at
               either airport.

                    CUT TO:
                    COCKPIT
                      TULLY
        Negative. We're landing in the Pacific.

                    CUT TO:
        INT. HONOLULU AIR TRAFFIC CONTROL
                     TOWER

EARHARDT
Roger dat. We prepare emergency crew.
(to Kona air traffic control) Kona, dis
Honolulu, we have Uniting Air Flight
1313 with bullet holes in cockpit
window. Dey no make it to airport and
dey try water landing just off your
coast. We need all emergency personnel
available to head for da aircraft. Wiki
wiki.

CUT TO:
INT. KONA AIR TRAFFIC CONTROL
TOWER
AIR TRAFFIC CONTROLLER WILLY
You got it, bruddah. (to emergency
crew) We got a swimmer.

CUT TO:
KONA COAST/EXT. KONA AIRPORT
Five emergency personnel paddle in from
surfing, run to the three fire trucks
and two ambulances, (in black and
white, fast forward, music in
background) drive in a few circles, and
(normal film) then run back to the
water with their surfboards.

CUT TO:
CABIN
EVAN
(to Randall)
What's going on?

                    RANDALL
      Let's just say you were right. The
            plane's going down.

                     TULLY
            (on public address system)
      Ladies and Gentlemen, we have had a
        minor incident in the cockpit.
      (Everyone looks worried) No need to be
      alarmed. There is no terrorist threat,
      (Everyone looks relieved) but we will
        need to make a minor detour to the
        Pacific Ocean. Flight attendants,
           prepare for water landing.

      Everyone screams. The oxygen masks drop
      down in the form of swimming mask and
                    snorkel.

                    CUT TO:
                  RIGHT WING
      Wing walker puts her hands on her face
      in fright and then holds on tightly to
                      wing.

                    CUT TO:
                  LEFT WING
      Parachutist also looks frightful and
                   jumps off.

                    CUT TO:
                    CABIN

(DING)
REBECCA
(on public address system)
Ladies and Gentlemen, the captain has
turned on the No Screaming sign.
(show sign, looks like Munch's *The
Scream*)

Everyone stops screaming for five
seconds and then resumes screaming.

CUT TO:
CABIN, REAR BATHROOM
Hugh opens the bathroom door and pulls
out Asian Man.

HUGH
Let's go. Back to your seat. The
plane's going down.

As they walk back toward their seats,
Ann peeks into the bathroom to make
sure Asian Man didn't pull any tricks.
She sees spelled out in pee: HELP.

TERI
(to Roberta)
I'm scared!

Roberta offers her hand. They hold
hands and lock eyes. They have a
moment. Roberta leans in to kiss Teri.

TERI
Not that scared.

288

CUT TO:
COCKPIT
The pilots are working hard to steady
the plane and to land closely to the
Kona coast. Wright is rapidly reading
through the emergency procedures
manual.

WRIGHT
It's all Chinese to me. (show manual—
written in Chinese) Should we get the
badminton player back in here to
translate?

TULLY
No, it's too late now. Larson, how are
we looking?

LARSON
Good, Captain. You're all lined up to
land half-mile off the Kona coast.

ROBERT HAYS (cameo) opens the cockpit
door from the cabin and pokes his head
in.
"I want to tell you . . . good luck.
We're all counting on you." (from
Airplane!)

CUT TO:
CABIN
REBECCA
(on public address system)
Ladies and Gentlemen, please prepare
for water landing.

Rebecca and Jan put on masks and
snorkels and brace themselves. All of
the passengers do the same.

CUT TO:
COCKPIT
Tully, Wright, and Larson are wearing
masks and snorkels.

TULLY
Five thousand feet. Four thousand feet.
Three thousand feet. Two thousand feet.
One thousand feet. Five hundred feet.
Brace!

CUT TO:
EXT. PLANE, VIEW FROM KONA
The plane lands safely, but bumpy, in
the ocean. The emergency crew watch
from their surfboards in the water.
When the plane comes to a stop the
emergency crew paddles to the plane.

CUT TO:
CABIN
Passengers look up hesitatingly and
then realize they're safe. Everyone
cheers.

JIMMY
(to Harold)
We made it, Daddy.

HAROLD
Yes, we did, son.

Teri powders her nose.

MARIE
(to Chrisall)
What are you doing?

CHRISALL
(Putting on sunscreen)
I burn easily. (shows front of bottle
to Marie) It's SPF albino . . . and
reef safe.

JAN
(on public address system)
Ladies and Gentlemen, now that we have
landed safely, it is time to evacuate.
Please leave all of your belongings,
grab your personal flotation device
that is located underneath your seat,
and head for the nearest exit.

All of the passengers on the left side
of the plane by the window and all of
the passengers on the right side of the
plane by the window, starting from the
front working backwards, stands, hits
his head, and drops back down. From
front to back it looks like dominos.

Cuban Husband looks at his wife in a panic, because he's handcuffed to the arm rest. How will he get out?! She nonchalantly slides the handcuff off of the arm rest. She smiles slyly, happy that if for only a brief moment in time she had control over him; he was the subservient one.

A passenger seated at the left side of the plane, by wing, opens the door and deploys the slide. The slide inflates within the plane. Many passengers wrestle with the slide and feel smothered by it. People are screaming. Randall walks up and shoots the slide, which rapidly deflates. The three passengers by that door push the useless slide out the door.

The passengers comply with Jan's announcement. Jan and Rebecca work the back door, and Brock and first class stewardess work the front door. Passengers next to the right wing exit try to get their door open, but the door is stuck.

CARPENTER
(seated next to the door by wing, grabs a cordless drill from his bag)
I knew this would come in handy.

He loosens the door and then uses his shoulder to push it open.

CUT TO:

EXT. PLANE

All three slides deploy on the right side of the plane and look like what you'd see at a water park: long shoot, curvy shoot, toilet bowl. People jump out, starting with Tully, Wright, and Larson at the front of the plane. Wright and Larson hold onto their personal rafts ('70s style with a cup holder).

Tully is treading water next to Wright and Larson, who are on their rafts.

                    TULLY
          (looks up at the plane)
      I knew I was forgetting something.

Most of the passengers are lounging on their rafts. The emergency personnel are paddling up. There are also four bartenders on stand-up paddleboards pulling mini-bars. There are six women (Greeters) in an outrigger passing out leis.

                   GREETERS
      Aloha. Welcome to Hawai'i. Aloha.
         Welcome to Hawai'i . . .

Passengers sip on margaritas and daiquiris with a miniature umbrella and pineapple wedge. Some passengers put on sunscreen. Teri and Roberta lie on rafts next to each other. Teri holds a reflective tanning panel up to her neck.

ROBERTA
(to Teri)
Are you trying to get skin cancer?!

TERI
I'm just working on my glow.

The guy with flares lights them and attaches them to his raft for decoration like they are tiki torches. One man fishes. The guy with the drone flies it over women, because he's a pervert.

CUT TO:
LUGGAGE COMPARTMENT
Door is open, Burt Bacharach plays a grand piano. He plays music for what now seems like a piano lounge.

CUT TO:
EXT. PLANE
Passengers continue to drop down the slides.

CUT TO:
OCEAN

294

Water Skier is set to be pulled.

                    WATER SKIER
                     Hit it!

Harold and Jimmy lie next to each other
on rafts. Jimmy's raft is child-size.

                      JIMMY
                   (to Harold)
             Daddy, are we there, yet?

                     HAROLD
Almost, son. We just need to wait our
turn to be rescued. How ya' feelin'?

                      JIMMY
                      Good.

                     HAROLD
               Were ya' scared?

                      JIMMY
                       No.

                     HAROLD
What ya' say we find some people to tip
                outta their rafts?

                      JIMMY
                      Yeah!

Evan and Randall lie next to each other
                 on their rafts.

                    RANDALL
                    (to Evan)
So, you have any other predictions,
              Sylvia Browne?

                     EVAN
I'm, uh, not actually psychic. My
    psychiatrist says that I'm—

                    RANDALL
It's OK. You don't have to tell me. I
              already know.

                     EVAN
We're going to be eaten by sharks. Did
you know that sharks can smell one part
per million of blood in the ocean? It's
   true. Look it up. Look it up.

                    RANDALL
Did you know that I once shot a deer at
  200 yards? Well, it was one of those
    cutout deers . . . and it was at a
  pistol range . . . but I shot it, and
   it fell over. A shark can't be that
              much different.

Rebecca lies on a door. It looks like a
scene from *Titanic*. Freezing air and
near-freezing water. She shivers and
holds onto Tully's hand. He's in the
                   water.

                    REBECCA
                  (to Tully)
                I'll never let you—

Bartender paddles up and offers Rebecca
a drink. She lets go of Tully's hand to
          grab the drink. He drowns.

                    REBECCA
       Oops. Well, that's what you get for
    cheating on me. And you think I didn't
                    know. Huh.

Morbidly Obese Woman sees yacht pull up
                    near her.

              MORBIDLY OBESE WOMAN
                  (to Lawyer)
        Help! Help! Are you here to save us?

                    LAWYER
      No. God, no. I don't want to get wet.
     Do you know how much this suit costs?
        Do I look like a lifeguard? I'm a
                    lawyer.

              MORBIDLY OBESE WOMAN
           Come on. Throw me a bone.

                    LAWYER
     By the looks of it you've already had a
                 full rack.

Lawyer throws a rib bone after he takes
               one more bite.

MORBIDLY OBESE WOMAN
No. I mean give me a break. Throw me a
lifesaver.

LAWYER
By the loo-. . . (under his breath)
that's too easy. (Out loud) Get closer.

Morbidly Obese Woman manages to get
closer to the yacht and Lawyer hands
her a business card.

LAWYER
Here's my card.

Lawyer's yacht pulls away.

Rescuer Jordan, different from Kona
rescuers, swims up to Morbidly Obese
Woman. He looks like he is with the
coast guard. It looks like a scene from
The Perfect Storm. Hurricane
conditions.

JORDAN
(to Morbidly Obese Woman)
Hi, I'm Jordan. I'll be your rescuer.

Chrisall and Marie lie next to each
other on life rafts.

CHRISALL
(to Marie)
Ah, this is the life, isn't it?

                    MARIE
If you consider surviving a plane crash
"the life," then I guess so. Now I know
that *this* is what my dream meant. Do
    you think we'll make the 5 o'clock
                    news?

                   CHRISALL
    Yeah. And 6 o'clock and 10 o'clock
   and . . . Have you ever noticed that
reporters and anchormen are starry-eyed
   when talking about plane crashes and
               other disasters?

                    MARIE
                    Yeah.

                   CHRISALL
    Look! Here comes a news crew now!

A cameraman and reporter Beverly paddle
    up in a two-person sea kayak.

                   BEVERLY
                 (to Marie)
             What happened?

                    MARIE
            The plane crashed.

                   BEVERLY
Yes, I see that. Do you have any idea
              of the cause?

                    MARIE
                  Gravity?

                    BEVERLY
                 (to Chrisall)
         How about you, Sir? Was this a
              terrorist attack?

                    CHRISALL
         If you call hummingbirds terrorists.

                    BEVERLY
         Hummingbirds? I don't understand.

                    CHRISALL
         I heard that there were hummingbirds in
         the cockpit that attacked and killed
                   the pilots.

                    BEVERLY
         (with a big smile on her face) The
         pilots died?! Someone died?! People
         died?! (clearing her throat and
         sounding serious) I'm sorry to hear
                     that.

         Chrisall punches Beverly and she falls
         out of the kayak. He shakes his hand
         and checks to make sure he didn't break
         a nail. Beverly comes up for air.

                    CHRISALL
                  (to Marie)
              Now *that's* starry-eyed.

                  CUT TO:
         CABIN

                     300

Spare Pilot is reading a magazine and doesn't even notice that the plane crashed. He's not wearing a mask and snorkel.

CUT TO:

OCEAN

Asian Man swims away from plane, making a mad dash for Asia. Hugh and Ann swim after him.

Camera pans back to show how far away Asia is from Hawaii.

Credits roll.

Credits pause.

CUT TO:

SAN JOSE AIRPORT UNLOADING ZONE, DUSK

Music playing: "No parking baby. No parking on the dance floor."

See Parking Cop dancing and singing and blowing his whistle.

Credits resume.

THE END

ABOUT THE AUTHOR

Entrepreneur and satirist Jeanne "Bean" Murdock brings a new approach to comedy, fusing observational humor with health and fitness knowledge. Performing on roller skates where she can, her improvised physical comedy is one that has never been done before. Jeanne's sassy, naive perspective wins audience attention, demanding that the show must go on.

As much as Jeanne loves to perform, she prefers writing. She is prolific, penning screenplays, books, and of course her own jokes, to name a few.

Originally from Cupertino, California, Jeanne was given the nickname **Bean** in third grade by her next-door neighbor simply because it rhymed with Jeanne. She studied physical education at Cal Poly and then started **BEAN**FIT Health and Fitness Services in 1992. Three years later, Jeanne was diagnosed with celiac disease, a condition that she included in her teachings. For 22 years she was a health and fitness professional who happened to be a comedian. Now, she is a comedian who happens to be a health and fitness expert.

Qualifications:
California Polytechnic State University, San Luis Obispo
Bachelor of Science in Physical Education
   concentration: commercial/corporate fitness
Graduation Date: June 1991

San Diego State University, San Diego, CA
Nutrition Didactic Program
Verified: May 2002

Questions? Comments? Please feel free to contact
Jeanne "Bean" Murdock anytime.

PO Box 372
Cornville, AZ 86325
Phone: 408-203-7643
Website: www.JeanneMurdock.com
E-mail: laugh@JeanneMurdock.com

Image edited by Greg Heller

Other books by Jeanne "Bean" Murdock
(via BEANFIT Publishing):

*The Every Excuse in the Book Book: How to Benefit from
     Exercising, by Overcoming Your Excuses*
*Successful Dating at Last! A Workbook for Understanding
     Each Other*
*It's Hard to Find Good Help These Days: A Customer
     Service Manual for Businesses*
*That's a Bunch of Quackery! How to Avoid Being
     Pick-pocketed by Misleading Claims in the Fitness
     Industry*
Serial Good Samaritan
Memorable Greetings
You Get the Picture
The Chew Crew: 3 books in 1

Co-author of Carole Breton's autobiography
My Guardian Angel Wears Antiperspirant
(Stinky Ghost Cat Books 2018)

Not-so ghost writer of Ted Gilbert's autobiography
Barefoot NOMAD
(POGA Publishing 2019)

Not-so ghost writer of Babe Daley's autobiography
Arizona Native
(Isley Publishing 2023)

www.ingramcontent.com/pod-product-compliance
Lightning Source LLC
Chambersburg PA
CBHW070551260626
47161CB00002B/573